Troubled Nate Thomas

T.N.T. Series, Volume 1

Lexy Timms

Published by Dark Shadow Publishing, 2016.

This is a work of fiction. Similarities to real people, places, or events are entirely coincidental.

TROUBLED NATE THOMAS

First edition. November 26, 2016.

Copyright © 2016 Lexy Timms.

Written by Lexy Timms.

Also by Lexy Timms

Alpha Bad Boy Motorcycle Club Triology
Alpha Biker

Conquering Warrior Series
Ruthless

Diamond in the Rough Anthology
Billionaire Rock
Billionaire Rock - part 2

Dominating PA Series
Her Personal Assistant - Part 1
Her Personal Assistant - Part 2
Her Personal Assistant - Part 3
Her Personal Assistant Box Set

Firehouse Romance Series
Caught in Flames
Burning With Desire
Craving the Heat
Firehouse Romance Complete Collection

Fortune Riders MC Series
Billionaire Biker
Billionaire Ransom
Billionaire Misery

Hades' Spawn Motorcycle Club
One You Can't Forget
One That Got Away

One That Came Back
One You Never Leave
Hades' Spawn MC Complete Series

Heart of the Battle Series
Celtic Viking
Celtic Rune
Celtic Mann
Heart of the Battle Series Box Set

Justice Series
Seeking Justice
Finding Justice
Chasing Justice
Pursuing Justice
Justice - Complete Series

Love You Series
Love Life: Billionaire Dance School Hot Romance
Need Love
My Love

Managing the Bosses Series
The Boss
The Boss Too
Who's the Boss Now
Love the Boss
I Do the Boss
Wife to the Boss
Employed by the Boss
Brother to the Boss
Senior Advisor to the Boss
Forever the Boss
Gift for the Boss - Novella 3.5

Moment in Time
Highlander's Bride
Victorian Bride
Modern Day Bride
A Royal Bride
Forever the Bride

R&S Rich and Single Series
Alex Reid
Parker

Saving Forever
Saving Forever - Part 1
Saving Forever - Part 2
Saving Forever - Part 3
Saving Forever - Part 4
Saving Forever - Part 5
Saving Forever - Part 6
Saving Forever Part 7
Saving Forever - Part 8

Southern Romance Series
Little Love Affair
Siege of the Heart
Freedom Forever
Soldier's Fortune

Tattooist Series
Confession of a Tattooist
Surrender of a Tattooist
Heart of a Tattooist

Tennessee Romance
Whisky Lullaby

Whisky Melody
Whisky Harmony

The Debt
The Debt: Part 1 - Damn Horse
The Debt: Complete Collection

The University of Gatica Series
The Recruiting Trip
Faster
Higher
Stronger
Dominate
No Rush

T.N.T. Series
Troubled Nate Thomas

Undercover Series
Perfect For Me
Perfect For You
Perfect For Us

Unknown Identity Series
Unknown
Unexposed
Unpublished

Standalone
Wash
Loving Charity
Summer Lovin'
Christmas Magic: A Romance Anthology
Love & College
Billionaire Heart

First Love
Frisky and Fun Romance Box Collection
Managing the Bosses Box Set #1-3

Troubled Nate Thomas
T.N.T. Series
Book 1
By Lexy Timms

Copyright 2016 by Lexy Timms

All rights reserved. No part of this publication may be reproduced, stored in or introduced into a retrieval system, or transmitted, in any form, or by any means (electronic, mechanical, photocopying, recording, or otherwise) without the prior written permission of both the copyright owner and the above publisher of this book.

This is a work of fiction. Names, characters, places, brands, media, and incidents are either the product of the author's imagination or are used fictitiously. Any resemblance to an actual person, living or dead, events, or locales is entirely coincidental. The author acknowledges the trademarked status and trademark owners of various products referenced in this work of fiction, which have been used without permission. The publication/use of these trademarks is not authorized, associated with, or sponsored by the trademark owners.

All rights reserved.
Copyright 2016 by Lexy Timms

TROUBLED NATE THOMAS

T.N.T Series

Part 1
Part 2
Part 3
COMING DEC 2016

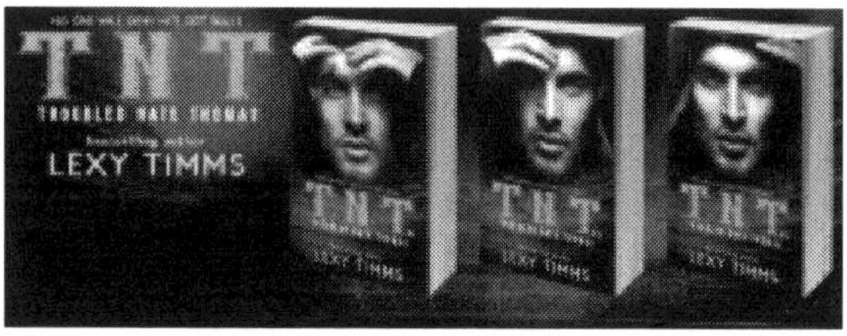
LEXY TIMMS

Find Lexy Timms:

Lexy Timms Newsletter:
http://eepurl.com/9i0vD
Lexy Timms Facebook Page:
https://www.facebook.com/SavingForever
Lexy Timms Website:
http://lexytimms.wix.com/savingforever

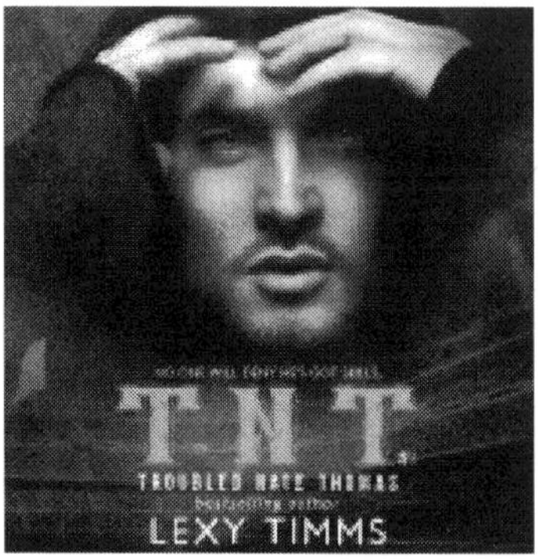
T.N.T.
TROUBLED NATE THOMAS
LEXY TIMMS

Description

Bestselling romance author, Lexy Timms, brings you a new sport romance series that'll blow your mind—it's dynamite!

"TNT" – Troubled Nate Thomas...

Dubbed so by the media because Nate's always getting into trouble. Talented, handsome, and halfway out the door, Nate Thomas is on his last chance with the Denver Broncos. No one will deny he's got skills—on the field and in the bedroom. However, his taste for the party lifestyle, his drinking, and his anger issues are putting his career in jeopardy.

Coach Johnson wants his starting quarterback to actually play the way his big-money contract states he can. He needs to find a way to get Nate's head back in the game. Threats, fines, and tickets don't seem to even slow Nate down.

With no choice but to try and risk the impossible, Coach Johnson hires a babysitter to look after Nate.

Amanda Jones is desperate for a job to help pay for her final year of her Master's. She's got a thesis to write and thinks being an au pair is the easiest way to get her work done, while making good money. She's stunned when she finds out she'll be taking care the infamous troublemaker, Nate Thomas, aka TNT.

The money's too good to say no to, but can she somehow convince this train-wreck of an athlete to get his crap together before they both destroy the one thing they're good at?

Chapter 1

A random "WHOOP" sounded every thirty seconds. Someone, somewhere, started it and it ran through the bar like the mating call of a wild frat brother. It was the only sound Amanda could hear over the blasting tech "music" that shook the walls and rattled the bottles behind the bar. They clapped together and danced, threatening to jump.

After half an hour of sitting here, she was starting to think jumping wouldn't be that bad of an idea. It was too bad the bar was on the ground floor.

The revelers danced, though to Amanda it looked like a coordinated seizure, trying not to hit each other. A couple was exploring each other's tonsils in the raised area behind the dance floor. Others were furiously dancing with themselves and randomly trying to relocate their partner. Amanda considered waiting for a break in the music, but she'd been waiting for a break in the music for over an hour. It was one continuous drumbeat that graciously allowed the occasional screaming guitar a moment or two in the sun.

"I SAID, WHAT. ARE. WE. DOING. HERE?" she screamed to be heard over the cacophony of music and conversation.

"We're having fun!" Amanda's roommate shot back, and slammed her beer down so fast it ran down her cheeks, split at her chin, and watered each breast separately through her thin t-shirt.

I had no idea, Amanda thought sarcastically. *So this is fun.* "Why..." she tried again. "WHY. AM. I. HERE?" She had to scream to be heard over the music.

"Because I'm too drunk to drive, silly!" Jennifer flashed her a smile before she leapt onto the dancefloor and began writhing to the pulsing music, her shirt clinging tightly across her chest. Two of the young men closest to her twisted and nearly tangled up in each other's legs as they tried to get to her. They both hit the floor. One turned the collision into a dance move while the other attempted to turn it into a fight.

Oh, now I get it. Designated driver is my *fun.* "I HAVE A JOB INTERVIEW IN THE MORNING!" Amanda screamed, but Jennifer wasn't listening. Amanda's protests were buried under the assault on her senses. *I cannot believe I let her talk me into this!* She mentally kicked herself. She had a fleeting thought where she wondered if it were possible to *actually* kick one's own ass and if so, how would it be arranged?

Jennifer was boy-crazy. No. That didn't begin to define it. She was a sex addict, in Amanda's opinion. How nice that she wanted to share it with Amanda tonight.

Amanda, on the other hand, was smart. Book smart, boring smart, all the kinds of things that went with a studious student. She figured that since she didn't have Jennifer's metamorphosed interest in boys, she tended to do things her roommate liked. Besides, Amanda never again planned to take Jennifer to a museum after the embarrassing recreation of *Nude Descending Staircase.* Amanda was still on probation.

There was a shift in the melee they called dancing, even the insufferable music stopped suddenly, and Amanda had to work her jaw to get her ears to pop in the sudden silence. For a moment she was relieved. Time stood still, for one glorious minute where people actually turned away from the dancefloor and moved back toward their tables or the bar. Conversation went down to normal speaking tones.

Then it got worse.

A whole lot worse.

As if the volume hadn't already been enough to keep half of Denver awake, a general scream rose from the crowd as a large good-looking man walked through the room, arms upraised, looking like he was not only reveling in the attention, but was directing it.

What was an assault on her senses became a tidal wave of noise and movement and flashing lights. And it was all directed around this newcomer. That alone was reason enough to dislike him. He gave off a wave of arrogance and self-importance. That was another.

Amanda found herself collecting reasons to not like the guy. She had no idea why she did. With his thick sandy hair, piercing blue eyes, and large ripped body, he surely belonged in the other column. The one marked "Reasons to make Amanda drool."

"TNT!" someone yelled. "TNT!"

Amanda prayed that the second time was an echo, but it was picked up as a chant across the room, out the door, across the street, and most likely into the next state. The light crowd suddenly doubled and tripled. It grew heavy enough that the chair Jennifer had been sitting in vanished, and the press of bodies was so thick Amanda was almost forced out of her chair as well.

The man pumped his fists up with each chant as he walked. No, he *paraded* up the room next to her and threw them down dramatically, ending the chant in wordless cheer and indecently overturning Amanda's table, which crashed into her arm, sending ice and diet Pepsi into an arc worthy of the Bellagio fountains that culminated on her blouse.

Oh, yes, right there. THAT'S the reason you don't like him.

"WET T-SHIRT!" The man, presumably TNT, yelled, then whooped and repeated it until it, too, became a chant. This one didn't end. His eyes, and for that matter, most of the others were fixed on her. Just a little south of her face.

"Come on, girl!" Amanda's roommate yelled and helpfully threw her beer on Amanda's chest. In her inebriated state, the glass slipped from her hand and flew into Amanda's face, sending her glasses into the midst of the gyrating crowd.

"JENNIFER!" Amanda screamed and dove for her glasses while trying to hold the fabric away from her breasts, thanking her mother and a conservative upbringing for the bra she wore under it. She scrambled under the table, spotting the glasses thankfully, though just out of reach. She lunged, just grabbing hold of one of whatever those plastic parts were that stuck out from the frame, when a pair of spiked heels crunched through the left lens. She pulled, but the heel was still in the middle of the frame. She reached out and swatted the ankle; the girl in the spike stilettos squealed and tripped. Amanda pulled her glasses free just in time to see the girl in question caught in the arms of the infamous TNT.

Her roommate screamed and Amanda half-turned, ready to calm her, to tell her that she was alright, that her glasses could be fixed, the frames were saved, but it wasn't Amanda's fate that had caused the scream. Jennifer had whipped off her shirt. She'd clearly had a very different upbringing, and was *not* wearing a bra. The blonde Amanda had tripped was similarly shirtless, but that was not entirely due to her own actions. The TNT person was waving her shirt around his head like a victory flag.

"BRONCOS! BRONCOS!" The chant had changed and several people pumped their fists and smashed cans on their foreheads. Some of the more Neanderthal-types body-slammed each other into walls. Somewhere a table crunched into kindling.

"I can't drive!" she told Jennifer. It might have been Jennifer; her vision was too blurry to be sure. The right lens was still intact, but with the other eye closed she still couldn't be sure. She was trying to stand while holding her shirt away from her body, and she only got so far before someone bumped into her and she went to her knees. Her face collided with TNT's crotch. When she pulled back, all she could see was a naked breast next to him and she had no idea who it belonged to.

Apparently, Mr. TNT did not necessarily care who was who, as one meaty hand descended and covered the naked breast, pulling it and the girl with it. He whooped again and grabbed both topless girls and pulled them to him. One of them had to be Jennifer, of course.

Amanda crawled to the edge of the dancefloor to find that her chair was gone, the table was gone, and the dancefloor had now expanded. She stood and pushed her way through the crowd which was increasingly topless, men and women both.

She pulled her cell phone from her purse while she fought her way out of the bar. It took longer than she would have expected given the size of the building. By the time she made it outside she needed the chill October air. It would help cool her temper. Or should have. It didn't work.

She made two calls, the first to a taxi, the second was to Jennifer's voice mail. In the first call she gave her name, current location, and destination. In Jennifer's voice mail she calmly said "Fuck you" and hung up. She didn't need this shit. Nobody did.

Chapter 2

"According to police reports, 'Troubled' Nate Thomas, known as TNT to his fans, proceeded to escort two naked women to a waiting limousine and from there moved to a house party in Lakewood hosted at the house of a teammate, Bronco's Center Nick Page."

"That's not true!" Nate objected. "They were NOT naked! They were only topless." He thought a moment. "And that's legal...I think."

"Shut up." The coach smacked him over the head with the newspaper he'd been reading. "The police were called sometime later when neighbors complained of a goat roasting in Mr. Page's driveway. According to the report, the goat was an entry in a 4H project by the neighbor's daughter who was subsequently found in Mr. Thomas's car, passed out drunk. She, too, was naked."

Coach Johnson tucked the paper under his arm. "You fucked a girl from 4H?" His face was purpling. It wasn't a good color on him. Nate had been seeing a lot of purple lately.

Nate shuffled his feet a touch uneasily. "No, no, that's all wrong, Coach. I swear. She was 19. The goat belonged to her little sister." He looked up.

No. Still purple.

"You ate her sister's goat?!"

"And the big sister." Nate grinned.

Coach Johnson hit him with the paper again. They stared at each other. Coach hit him again. "We do *not* need this! We do NOT need to keep bailing your sorry ass out of jail at three in the morning because you were caught skinny dipping in the reflecting pool at the Lincoln Memorial."

"We won that game, Coach."

"We didn't win the game in Minnesota when you lined up five naked cheerleaders for your own ski jump practice in your hotel room!"

"Bobsled," Nate corrected, smiling. Damn, that was a good story.

Coach hit him again. "How do you justify what happened in Los Angeles?"

Nate held up his hands, palms out. "Ok, that's not fair, that question is not fair. You know I don't remember anything after I dropped my pants on the Walk of Fame. I do remember that Fred Astaire had tiny feet, though."

Coach Johnson raised the newspaper again and held it over Nate's head, who closed his eyes and waited for the blow. Instead the coach tossed the paper onto the floor in disgust.

Nate opened one eye to see if the coast was clear. Satisfied that no more attempts were going to be made on him with a rolled-up newspaper, he opened the other one.

The floor was still wet from the showers. Wet towels piled up around the lockers and the paper soaked up the water and the words bled and blurred and water mixed with ink to create a brown soup. For a moment he saw his own face, grinning. Girls with the good bits greyed out. Then the image dissolved. Gone.

"The press had dubbed you 'Troubled', and instead of learning from it, correcting it, you embrace it like a friggin' badge of honor."

Nate blinked. Was his coach joking? "It is!"

"No, it ISN'T!" Coach Johnson ran a hand down his face and made a fist. "You're an embarrassment to this team. You're a bomb waiting to go off! And you are a *disgrace* to the game of football! You're supposed to be professional! This frat boy shit has got to go."

"Coach, I show up for practice and for each game sober and ready to give it everything I've got. You know that. We don't win every game, but we win most of the them, and I'm the reason we win most of them." Nate grinned. "Well. Mostly."

That didn't seem to be the right answer either. Coach just looked...sad. Frustrated. He shook his head, and for a moment Nate felt a twinge of uneasiness.

It was better when Coach was purple. He knew what to do with that.

This...This was a lot more complicated.

"You're a good player, Nate. One of the best. You could be great, one of those who becomes a legend, but all you're gonna leave behind is a legend of stupid shit mistakes that'll make you the laughingstock of professional football. You do good work on the field, hell, I put you as the starter because you put everything you have on the field every day. But you don't have much, Nate. You spend it all on girls and booze, and there's nothing left for the game."

"I'm the best quarterback in the league." Nate shot back, going from uneasy to angry in an instant.

Coach Johnson gave him a look that was usually reserved for the last quarter of the game when the score was down. All fire. "Don't use that quote on me, son; it was created by the owner of this team to get more people to the games."

Nate crossed his arms. "If I'm such a lost cause, why isn't *he* reaming me out?"

It could have been meant as a slight, a dig, but Johnson knew it for what it was, an honest question. "You're a monkey, Nate. You're a trained monkey with a tin cup and when the owner plays his organ grinder, you dance in front of the crowds with your hat and cup and people laugh at you and put dimes in your cup. They come to laugh at you, Nate. But they come, they fill the seats, and that's all any owner wants."

"I AM NOT A LAUGHINGSTOCK!" Nate bellowed as he jumped to his feet. "I'm the best quarterback in the league!"

Coach Johnson said nothing. The gaze he gave his player was hard and full of...sadness? Again?

That uneasy feeling came back. Nate looked at him long and hard. Swallowed hard before asking, as if that would get rid of the sudden lump in his throat. "I'm not?"

"Nate," Coach sighed, "I'm not letting you play next week. Sanderson's going to start."

"Sanderson?" Nate scoffed. "I'm way better than Sanderson."

"You used to be, Nate. Sanderson's been working while you've been whoring. He's catching up to you. Be careful he doesn't leave you in the dirt."

For the first time since signing the contract for pro-ball, Nate Thomas was scared. "What about my contract?" he asked in a smaller voice than he could ever remember using in this room. He looked around at the lockers, inhaled the familiar scents of sweat and adrenaline and everything else that went into a locker room.

Fear didn't belong in this room. There was no place for it.

Coach shrugged. "It doesn't say anything about how many times you play in a season," he said, his tone gruff. Dead serious. "And Mr. Bancroft's attorneys drew up that little gem. Ask yourself if they didn't leave a little wiggle room for them to wriggle out of."

Nate thought for a moment. "I guess I don't know, Coach. Maybe I'm the wrong one to ask."

"You're not playing next week, Nate. You're benched until further notice."

Benched? Benched.

THAT didn't happen to Nate Thomas.

And just like that the fear was gone. A fist came out. Smashed into the locker next to him hard enough to leave a dent. "How long is that?" Nate yelled, resisting the urge to punch another locker only because his hand hurt like hell, except he wasn't about to admit that to anyone.

"Until you can show me that you're a grown-up. When you can prove you're no longer holding onto college and all-night keggers and parades of naked girls. You play again when you grow up and not a damn minute before."

Nate took a breath. Took another.

You gotta calm yourself down. Aren't you proving his point? Stop it...Breathe. Like before the Super Bowl. This is just another game. Just...a different kind.

Breathe.

"Come on, Coach." Nate said quietly when he had himself reined in enough to look contrite. To even mean it. Mostly. "Come on, please! Football is all I have; I don't know nothing else."

"I don't know *anything* else." Coach muttered half under his breath.

"Then you know how I feel!" Nate grabbed the other man's arms. "Please. Don't make me miss the games."

"We're hiring you a babysitter, Nate," Johnson said. "Someone trained to handle aberrant and childish personal...it...ty."

Whatever the coach was going on about, Nate wasn't listening. A girl had just come through the door, tall and insecure. An interesting combination, as she came in holding her shoulders back like she was trying to appear confident, when the face behind the glasses was all scared rabbit.

He'd seen her somewhere before. *Where...?*

"HEY!" Nate yelled it the second he realized who she was. "WET T-SHIRT!" He waved enthusiastically at the pretty girl who stuttered in through the double doors.

"Um... excuse me..." She held up a piece of paper and looked at Coach Johnson. "I think I must be at the wrong address."

Coach leaned in close to Nate. Spoke right in his ear, his voice low. Deadly. No one who heard Coach talk like that forgot it. The last time he'd heard that voice, it was the third down on the fourth quarter and Coach had been telling Nate to throw long. They'd been down by six. And Nate had messed it up anyway.

He'd been kind of hungover. Maybe.

Not a pleasant memory.

"That's your babysitter, Nate. Don't fuck it up. If she quits, you're out. I'll make sure you get suspended indefinitely."

Wait, what? Babysitter? Nate snorted. "No problem, Coach," he said and turned his award-winning smile on the mismatched-dressed girl in the ugly glasses, who had lost the confident shoulders and was now timidly crossing the room, looking around like she was expecting to be attacked from all sides.

"You stay away from me!" she snapped, and pointed at Nate.

Coach Johnson stepped between them and held out his hand. "I'm Miles Johnson," he said, "but most folks in this room call me 'Coach'. Please, step into my office, Miss..."

"Jones," she finished, and looked around him with an expression that was more disgust than anything. Coach looked over his shoulder. Nate flicked his hair back and grinned so broadly, his face hurt.

"You look like a bad rendition of the Joker from Batman. Heath Ledger did it with more sex appeal." He shook his head in disgust and turned toward Scared Rabbit, holding open the door to his office with a broad sweeping gesture and courtly bow. "My office, if you please."

"Ah... I guess?" She half-walked, half-ran to the designated office with Nate smiling broadly after her.

Joker. Yeah, right.

"STAY!" Coach ordered and shut the door.

Man, was he pissed.

Nate grinned until the girl was out of sight and then massaged his sore cheek muscles. With a little make-up, a bit less clothing, some nice heels... she wouldn't be so bad.

Yeah, he reached into his locker and grabbed a bottle of cologne. *This was in the bag.*

The bottle fell from his grip and shattered at his feet.

Chapter 3

"I think there's been a mistake." Amanda sat down cautiously, paranoid the chair was going to explode out from under her. It might. You never knew. It had been that kind of a day.

"I think there has." Coach Johnson countered, giving her an all-over kind of look that made her feel more than a little uncomfortable. The man was old enough to be her father. "I was expecting someone... older and less... attractive."

"I'm sorry?" Amanda asked. "What do my age or appearance have to do with my qualifications?"

"I only meant..."

"I know what you meant and, frankly, I'm a bit offended by it. It's bad enough to have to deal with that..." She pointed out the office window where Nate was alternating smiling and flexing in front of a mirror. "But to have my qualifications contingent on physical appearance is rather sexist and upsetting."

"I don't think—"

"No, I believe that you did. I'm currently working on my Master's thesis in child psychology. I'm experienced as a nanny and an au pair, though there's not a lot of difference. I've managed children of every age, and regardless of my height, weight or age, I am more than qualified."

"It's just that—"

"And plus, this is a live-in position, is it not?" Amanda continued, crossing her arms and leveling him with a glare.

He shifted uneasily. "A separate suite, yes, but..."

"Then it's perfect, as my roommate and I are currently looking for a new place to live. Rather, I'm looking for a new place; she's looking for a new roommate. It's better that way. So, you need me. I need the job, and the timing is perfect. Now that we have established that my 'looks' and age are no longer pertinent, I would like to start right away. Is that all right with you?"

Coach Johnson hesitated for a moment, looking much like a first-grader who wasn't altogether sure whether it was his turn to talk yet. "Yes?"

"Are you asking me or telling me?" Amanda sighed. They never grew up, did they? Perpetual little boys. She shook her head. "No matter." She smiled, leveling him with another glare as he seemed about to protest it. Darn it, she needed this job and some oversized Phys. Ed. teacher in gym shorts wasn't going to get in her way. "I'm sure we'll get along splendidly. Now, when do I get to meet the child?"

Coach Johnson pointed through the window. His hand shook slightly.

Amanda jumped to her feet, feeling the blood drain from her face. "You left the child out there in the locker room? Alone with that... that... ape?"

"It *is* the ape. You've been hired to get him under control and keep him out of the press."

Amanda pointed.

Nate was slamming his shoulder into a wall and yelling, "DEFENSE!"

"Him?"

Coach nodded.

"There's been some mistake," Amanda said, shaking her head and backing up toward the door to the office. "I'm sorry, but that..."

"Ape?" Coach supplied helpfully.

"Thank you, is not a child!"

Nate was playing on his phone and yelling, "JUMP! JUMP! JUMP!"

"Well, I mean by age."

"Listen. Nate's a really good player; he could be great..." He paused, his gaze flicking over her body again, seeming to notice for the first time the tailored suit she'd painstakingly pressed only that morning. "Ok, you probably don't care about sports, I figured that much out on my own. I need you, I need someone. So does he, although he doesn't know it. He's got a gift, a gift that's worth a lot of money to a lot of people. They've catered to him all his life, let him get away with things because of that gift." Coach walked to the chair in front of his desk and sat, indicating that Amanda take the other again. "These people put a lot of money into him, and they're going to get it back with interest. If he can play well, they make a little back. If he can play well and be a clown, they make a lot more back. He becomes a sideshow freak."

Amanda sat and crossed her legs. Was she seriously considering this? No, she'd be a fool. "It's really..."

"Not your problem, yes, I know. But he could be good enough to make them all lots of money on their investments, if the wild streak doesn't end him first."

"I can't..."

"I understand that," Coach said. "But he needs a nanny or his career will end. And soon. Then all the people who fawn over him now will forget him and leave him alone. He's never been alone."

The picture of an abandoned little boy crying by the side of the road came to mind. Wearing a football jersey.

It was beyond pathetic.

And yet...

No.

No, I can't. Say it, girl, and get out of here.

"No, I...."

"And," Coach said, leaning forward a little, his tone wheedling. "You and your roommate are looking for other accommodations. This is a full suite. Separate from the main house with its own locks and a separate alarm system."

"Whose house?" Amanda didn't wait for an answer. She knew. Of course she knew. "His?! Doesn't he already have all the codes to his own house?"

"Coach?" Nate yelled through the window, causing Amanda to jump in her chair. "I'm tweeting!" He chuckled a bit at that as if he'd been inordinately clever. "What's the word for doing the same thing all the time, first thing first, then the next one, and then the next one, and then... you know..."

"Systematic?" Amanda asked, not sure why she was even answering.

"YEAH! Uh, how do you spell that? P.A.T.H.E.T.I.C.A.L?"

"Yeah, Nate, that's it," Coach said, giving her a look loaded with meaning. "Give us a bit, will you?"

Nate winked. "Got it, Coach, you old dog, you!"

Coach sighed and looked at Amanda. "The thing is, he tests high in every IQ test he's ever had. Even though he sounds like an idiot. He's not. No one's ever made him think. He's never had to stand on his own two feet. When he gets dumped at the end of his career..."

"He'll be worth millions?"

"He's telling the world he has a 'pathetical' style. How long do you think his money will last?" Coach looked at her. "Please?"

This is a bad idea.

"I do need to find a place to live right away..."

Amanda instinctively caught the keys Coach tossed her. "We'll sign the paperwork later. I'll have legal draw up something impressive. Two...no, three times your usual fee..."

Amanda sat staring at the keys without blinking.

"Nate!" Coach called through the door. "Come meet your new nanny!"

Nate leaned on the doorframe and looked at her. "Wow, thanks Coach, but I can get my own girls. She's cute, but she just doesn't do it for me."

Coach opened his mouth, but Amanda had quite honestly had enough. If she was doing this, she was doing it RIGHT. What was one more disobedient little boy in her line of work?

She stood up, crossed her arms and faced him, nose to nose as it were. "I don't know what passes for thinking in that caveman-thick skull you use for a battering ram, you low-level, knuckle-dragging hormone, but you will talk TO me, NOT about me when I am *sitting right there*. And you WILL talk politely to me out of respect for a human being who is more highly evolved than your life single-cell life form!"

"Coach?" Nate asked. His voice rose on the end of the word, eyes wide and somewhat panicked.

"What she said was that you're going to be nice to her, or you can't play. You're benched for the season until this girl says differently."

Nate shoved past Amanda. Slammed his hands down on Coach's desk hard enough to make the pens rattle in the coffee mug they were kept in. "You can't do that!"

"According to your contract, I can!" Coach said, leaning back, arms behind his head, the picture of a man at ease.

"You didn't read the contract?" Amanda asked, trying very hard not to laugh. It wouldn't do to snicker at one's charge.

"Coach!"

"She's staying in your guesthouse, Nate."

Nate blinked a few times. Frowned. "Ok, I'll buy a new goat!"

"What goat?" Amanda looked from one to the other.

Coach shook his head. "It's not about the goat, Nate."

"What goat?"

"This is it. You're off the team until this little lady says otherwise!"

"I'm not comfortable with that," Amanda said, thinking about slamming her own hands down on the desk if it got his attention. So far nothing else seemed to be working.

"You don't have to determine his ability to play," Coach said with a shrug. "Just keep him out of trouble."

"No, I mean being called 'little girl'," she said, flexing her fingers as making a fist at one's new boss probably wasn't advisable. And would get her laughed out of the room in all likelihood.

"I stand corrected," Coach said with a solemn nod.

"Well, I'm not sitting down for this!" Nate shoved past Amanda for a second time, and paused in the doorway. He had no problems with making a fist at his boss at all it seemed. He even used it, pounding on the doorframe. "I'm taking this to the general manager."

"Go ahead, Nate. My contract says I can do whatever I want. I read mine."

Nate growled, spun on one heel, and left.

Coach stood and held out his hand. "Welcome to the Denver Broncos," he said.

Chapter 4

They weren't kidding with the word "suite." The place was bigger than the apartment she'd been sharing with Jennifer. The key difference? This was supposedly all hers. Furnished, and awesome.

It was way more space than she needed, not that she wasn't going to revel in it. With two large bedrooms, a living room, small kitchen and even a tiny nook off the living room just the right size for an office. She was almost numb as she went from room to room, shaking her head in wonder as she stared. There was no way to use all that space. Even if she totally spread out.

And furnished. Who did that? Granted, the main room was predominantly white; which went a long way to proving her charge never entered the premises. Her charge. A grown boy needing a sitter. What the heck were the Broncos going to tell the media? She ran a hand along the white leather coach. Just like a real small child, Nate probably couldn't keep things white for very long.

She made a bunch of trips to the rental truck, but the living room was simply too nice to clutter with cardboard. She stacked her boxes, most of which had *BOOKS* scrawled on them in marker, into the room she designated as the spare. It was sweaty work and she was ready for a break by the time she finished.

The bathroom had to be her favorite room. She stood and stared for a long time at the massive tub with some kind of Jacuzzi arrangement, not altogether sure she could manage turning it on without an advanced degree in engineering. The rugs were royal blue, going with the white and silver theme of the room which was bigger than her bedroom growing up. She sank up to her ankles in the deep piled plush next to the shower while she examined the controls there, wide-eyed. You could hold a small, though intimate, party in there, with no one getting left out in the cold. Between the giant showerhead coming down seemingly from the ceiling, and the multiple jets on every side, getting washed was simply a matter of standing still. Somewhat like a carwash for humans. She dropped her towel and entered cautiously, eyes wide.

She never wanted to leave.

Imagine how much better this would be with company...

Red-faced, she unwrapped a brand-new loofah and lathered herself with perhaps a little more force than necessary, trying to scrub the image of the amazing, troublesome Nate from her brain.

Seriously, it wasn't working.

How could it? The space was too luxurious...too...much.

To be honest, so was he.

By the time she stepped out, her skin had been scrubbed raw and her cheeks were pink with embarrassment. The only bonus would have been no way to see just how stupidly he had her riled up. Ironically, there were mirrors everywhere, and despite the steam she pretty much had a 360-degree view of the blush that crept all the way down to her breasts.

With a groan, she threw the towel on the floor and stomped naked into the bedroom and threw herself on the bed.

Which was, of course, beyond amazing.

"What am I doing here?" She lay with her forearm over her eyes, thinking of all the ways this was a really, *really* bad idea. She even found a few lame reasons why she ought to just pack up and leave right now. Only, as duly noted already, the bed was amazing, and the room was amazing, the shower beyond anyone's dreams, the house was amazing...and the money—

That money went beyond amazing. She could finish her year of school. Pay off her credit card debt. Hell, she might even be able to afford to go home for Christmas if she could somehow finagle the time off.

Okay, so she'd stay. For now.

She got up and found her jeans and a long-sleeved t-shirt with a unicorn on it. The fact that it was pooping rainbows was entirely her business. No one had said anything about a dress code.

Clothes decided, she'd just gone to make a cup of tea when there came a knock on the door.

Nate Thomas stood on her stoop, wide sloppy grin and all.

"Hey there!" he said and gave a perfunctory wave with all four fingers flying in separate directions.

"Hey there?" Amanda echoed back.

"Can I come in?" He looked past her into her new home.

"Sure..." Amanda hesitated, but it *was* his house, after all. He probably had the right to see what she'd done with it.

Nate walked into the living room and looked around, and then gave a low appreciative whistle. "This is nice," he said with a lot more enthusiasm than was really merited. "I really like it, it's so.... White."

"Well, it's yours," Amanda laughed, thinking she really should have done more with it. Maybe added some of her personal mementoes.

"No, I couldn't do that, you stay here." Nate waved her off.

Amanda blinked. "No, I mean, it's literally yours. You own it."

"Oh," Nate smiled and nodded. "Because it's on my land. I get it. Very funny!" He smiled and nodded again.

He seemed to be stuck on the two reactions. She was starting to wonder what he would do if she told him the house was on fire. Smile? Nod? He played pro football, he couldn't be that dumb, right?

"What can I do for you Mr. Turner?" Amanda asked, not wanting to actually know the answer. Anything to keep from descending into the world of eye-rolling. She was a professional. Professionals didn't roll their eyes.

"I was just thinking..." Nate said slowly, his forehead creasing into a pretty frown.

"Were you?"

"I was just thinking, you told Coach that you needed a place to live and that you were still studying for something in school..."

"I'm working on my Master's thesis in abnormal—"

"Yeah, that." He waved his hand. "Anyway, it occurred to me that if you tell Coach I'm ready to play, you could just stay on here for as long as you wanted. You know, the electric and all that's paid anyway. No need for you to leave. You could stay here and study for... oh, say a year?"

Amanda blinked. Now she was the one stuck on auto-play reactions. "Mr. Turner," she said carefully, wondering just how much of this was going to have to be explained before it penetrated that thick skull. "You know I can't do that. I have to report to Mr. Johnson—"

"Who?"

Amanda sighed. "Coach."

"Oh! Right."

"I have to report to Mr. ... uh, 'Coach' as I see fit. Having heard some of your exploits, not to mention having the pleasure of witnessing them first-hand, I can't say that I don't understand his point of view." She crossed her arms, leveled him a glare. "Besides, there's something you need to know about me. Bribes are *not* acceptable behavior. Ever."

"What if I told you to leave?" Nate shot back.

"Then I'd appreciate you helping me load the truck, since it's here." She shrugged. "You won't be playing again this year, though. That's in the contract."

He took a half step back, as if she'd struck him. His face even seemed to pale slightly, and for a moment she wondered if football players ever fainted.

No, he wasn't that fragile. If anything, he seemed angry.

"I can't take the year off! Don't you get that? They leave me on the side, I'll be traded. They'll forget about me." He shook his head and glared at her. "You can't do this. You've got not right—"

"Who are 'they'?" Amanda asked, seeing past the fury to the fear, the confusion in his eyes.

"Them! The fans, the... the girls! If I'm out for a while year, then I'll be forgotten. They'll focus on someone else, someone like Sanderson, and he's... he's freakin' boring. The dude can't play!" He shoved past her, pacing around the room, half raising a fist that for a moment caused her to flinch. Well, up until he clocked himself in the forehead with it. It had to hurt, though he gave no sign of that as he stopped dead in front of her and put out his hands, capturing her shoulders and giving her a shake hard enough to rattle her teeth. "So, here's the deal. You get the place here rent-free for the season, you tell Coach that I'm behaving, and everyone wins."

"No." Amanda raised her arms, knocking his hands free, and stepped back. Scared little boy or not, there were boundaries.

"Oh, come on, you don't want to do this anymore than I do. This is stupid. I don't need a babysitter!"

"Good!" Amanda crossed her arms. Stared him down—rather, up at him. "Now you just have to prove that and we can all go home."

"I am home," Nate muttered.

She rolled her eyes. "You know what I mean."

"No. This is ridiculous." Nate crossed his arms.

Amanda tried not to notice how thick and large they were. Tried not to remember how it felt when he'd held her trapped... not trapped; he just hadn't realized his own strength. It hadn't hurt, it'd felt—she pushed the thought away. He'd let her go the second she'd moved away.

"Am I missing something?" There was an odd pleading note in his voice.

Amanda's stomach clenched. *I will not fall for this.*

She looked at the square jaw, the large, heavy arms, the shoulders that looked sculpted from a Redwood. *Hell no!* she thought, and put a heavy leash on that thought.

Whatever he said next, she missed it entirely. One minute he was there huffing about something or another, and then suddenly the door was slamming shut behind him. She watched him through the window, stomping across the lawn to the big house only a short distance away.

It was only a matter of time before he came back.

Amanda lunged for the door, and locked it tight with slightly shaky hands.

Why can't I keep my head on my shoulders? He's a client, dammit!

"Yeah, when was the last time you had a 'client' who was more than six years old?" she muttered as she dropped down on the couch and stared straight ahead at the television without turning it on. She sat there, fuming at the man, the job, at Jennifer, at herself for taking the job.

Which led down a whole new rabbit hole of self-hatred. Seriously. Here she was, babysitting the man her ex-roommate had slept with. She'd probably been all over those thick, heavy arms, been wrapped in the muscles, felt those big, heavy hands caress her breasts, stroke her legs. She imagined that Jennifer would have shimmied out of the skirt she was barely wearing. Amanda had seen the way Nate's large, capable hands had covered the girl's breast.

Don't forget, it wasn't just one girl, was it? There's been that other one...whatever her name was.

Yeah. The one who'd destroyed Amanda's glasses. Which brought her back to why the whole thing had started. The wet t-shirt contest.

What was so wrong that she, Miss Amanda Jones, should be so mortified that her shirt was wet? Everyone else was so uninhibited.

She knew exactly why. In a perverse way Amanda was jealous; not that she wanted Nate. Certainly not. He was disgusting.

But to be that open, that free... To be that bold and whip her shirt off in a crowd and feel someone's strong, capable hands pulling at her tender skin... to feel his hot breath on her neck, the way he would nibble at her nape and make her feel beautiful.

She caught herself. Beauty wasn't everything. Brains got you further. Brains kept with you into old age when beauty fades. But still, just once, would it be so bad to be... well, so bad?

Unzipping her jeans and reaching into her panties, she imagined it was... not *him*. It was someone else, someone she could respect and admire, someone who held her that way, owned her, claimed her as his own.

She would stand exposed, covered by his hands, under his protection, his love. And later, in the car—a stretch-limo of course—she would be completely naked as he ravished her, first with his eyes and then with short breaths. Caught by her beauty, he'd reach for her. There'd be desire and passion, and even respect at her boldness.

How he, not Nate, *definitely not* Nate, but 'he' would hold her, his hands running down her side, cupping her breasts, grabbing her ass in strong handfuls and taking her wet sex to his face.

And Amanda—shy, introverted Amanda—would lewdly and wantonly writhe in the back of the stretch- limo as it drove through the night, shamelessly attached to his lips, tongue, teeth as he worked over her more intimate place. His tongue flashing over her clit, delving into her hot sex, and he would bring her close, so close.

She would beg him for release, but he would turn her around then, on all fours, and she would hear his zipper and anticipate him. She would feel his hardness slide into her, feel the fullness of his shaft opening her, and driving deep, so deep.

She would take great handfuls of the carpeting and cry out as he took her; she would feel impaled, filled, taken, and he would keep driving into her. Then he would pull back again, ramming that fullness, driving the thickness into her again and again.

Her orgasms would wash over her, one after another, and the whole time he would continue to use her and take her, his shaft swelling and pulsing with his own impending release.

She would take him then, ride him while he spent himself in her heat. She'd still be shaking and pulsing from her orgasms, so many... And when he came it would be deep inside of her, and his pulsing would become hers and her pulsing would become his. They would lie, spent and sated on the floor of a car.

Oh...yes...Much like...that...

Amanda gasped. Then screamed.

Her flying fingers had found her own orgasm, had made her legs tremble. She suppressed another scream as a second wave tore through her. She bent over her hand as she spasmed, nearly falling off the couch in her intense release.

Then realization hit.

That single scream that had escaped her lips sounded suspiciously like *Nate*.

She lay there, fingers wet, panting and trying to catch her breath.

She had just enough air to say two words.

"Oh shit..."

Chapter 5

"Coach Johnson," Amanda said, and thought she was doing pretty well when she managed to find a smile. "How are you?"

"May I come in?" Coach Johnson asked. He didn't look happy. So far she'd never seen him happy. Perhaps he never was and there was nothing to worry about.

Then why was her stomach full of butterflies trying madly to escape?

It wasn't like she had anything to worry about anymore. Hadn't she already moved past caring somewhere around 5am? This...*This* was just icing on the cake.

"Sure." Amanda shrugged and stood aside. "Why not."

"Rough night?" When he asked, he sounded as though he cared.

Why did he have to go and do that?

She's been prepared for him to yell. To get angry. To even throw things. But this fatherly kindness left her rather...well...knocked over. Now here she was, a grown woman, realizing that some small part of her wanted to curl up in his arms and suck her thumb and say it was too hard, that she couldn't do it, but could she keep the guesthouse? It was a small voice and she ruthlessly stamped it out, but it didn't stay quiet long.

Besides wasn't there some saying about how the best defense was a good offense?

For a moment she was proud that she'd picked up so much football knowledge. Then she remembered she was supposed to be mad.

Really mad.

She turned on him before he'd even gotten through the doorway. "It's like living with a Neanderthal!" she thundered. "He had women over last night. All night! The music was so loud no one in the area got any sleep, and by that I mean *me*." She waved off the objection that Coach wasn't making. "No, I checked, they were both of age, at least physically, but one of them came to the house holding a teddy bear in a nightgown."

Coach chuckled, standing with his arms crossed like he was ready to take on the entire defensive line. "The way you said that, it sounds like the teddy bear was wearing a nightgown."

She gave him a level look. "It was. At first. Then next thing I knew she'd stripped and put that teddy bear's nightgown on like it was hers! Seriously! It didn't cover much, let me tell you. Wasn't waterproof either. It completely disappeared in the pool, except for the piece that ended up clogging the pool filter so that it ran at a high-pitched cry all night. Which, in turn, had all the dogs in the neighborhood howling."

"I take it you could hear it, too?"

"NO! I HEARD THE DOGS!" She closed her eyes and counted to ten. Backward. Substituting swear words for the numbers. "I'm sorry, I'm just so exhausted."

He clucked in sympathy. "It sounds like a rough night."

She leveled a glare at him. "That was the start. Apparently, the meal choice for naked houseguests is to grill sausage in the pool."

"The grill was in the pool." It wasn't a question.

"They float after a fashion." It was her turn to cross her arms. Meeting his gaze squarely, eye to eye. Neither flinched. "It was comforting to know that the fire department only takes ten minutes to respond to a grass fire in this neighborhood."

He cleared his throat. "That's the sort of thing you were hired to prevent, Ms. Jones."

"Well, I gave them a phony name, but they knew whose house this was. I had to tell them that Nate was away at training camp and I started the fire because I don't like flowerbeds. So at least it won't be in the papers... At least, I don't think."

His head tilted back, eyes closed. It was his turn to count to ten. She could hear him. He was a better man than her. He was actually using numbers. "Thank you," he said quietly.

She sighed. "Again, I'm sorry, I didn't sleep last night at all. I'm cranky." She straightened and made an effort to try and smile. "What can I do for you?"

"How about we wait till Nate gets here?" He headed toward the couch and sat down, motioning for her to do the same.

A chill shot through her. Pure panic. "Why is... Why's Nate coming?"

"Because I told him to meet us here," he replied as though it was obvious.

"There is no way you're going to get him out of bed this morning, Coach," she muttered, and sat, arms still crossed. Knowing she'd gone from power position to pouting child, she didn't care at this point. "With the antics he pulled last night, it took me half an hour to load him on a wheelbarrow and roll him up to his room. It would've been longer if he hadn't passed out, lying over the thick branch by the front door. Good thing that tree's an oak; I highly doubt it would have held him otherwise. Who knows why he was climbing the thing at the time. Anyway, I parked the wheelbarrow right under his knees and pushed him backward."

He stared at her a long moment. She swore the corners of his lips were twitching. "Where did you find a wheelbarrow?"

"Gardener's shed. It wasn't exactly clean. Did he ever have horses?"

Coach's lips curled upward. "No, but I'm sure they use fertilizer."

"Good." She reveled in the image a moment.

"I'm sure your second night here will be better."

Was he *laughing* at her?

She shook that thought off. "I don't see how you're going to get him here. You won't see him this side of the pit for most of the—"

A knock at the door interrupted her.

"You want to get that, or should I?" Coach asked finally when she hadn't moved.

She broke from her reverie, shaking her head in confusion before getting up and opening the door.

"Mornin'!" Nate called, and pushed past her into the room. "Hey, Coach!"

Nate was fresh, active, and, to all appearances, bursting with energy.

I hate him.

She sighed and a single sob escaped her lips as she closed the door. She lay her head on it a moment before turning finally to face the men. Only, neither seemed to have even noticed her momentary lapse. Nate had crashed on the couch next to Coach, and was playing with the bowl of mixed nuts she'd left out on the coffee table. He cracked a walnut in his fist.

The sound was like a rifle shot to her throbbing head.

Amanda gritted her teeth and returned to her spot, sitting somewhat gingerly, when what she really wanted to do was to wrap her hands around Nate's neck and see if she could make him sit still for a while. Or permanently. Either would work at this point.

"Next game's in L.A.," Coach Johnson said without preamble, his eyes on Nate's face. "Since you're coming along," he turned toward Amanda briefly, gesturing with his thumb, "we have to find an excuse for you being there and hanging around this guy." He jerked his thumb at Nate.

Amanda followed his hand motion, slowly letting the words sink in. Her brain seemed sluggish, but she thought he'd just said something about her needing to travel...with Nate? She cleared her throat. "Wait, I'm going to L.A.?"

Both men looked at her. She was starting to get used to confused stares. It was kind of what you'd expect people to look like if you suddenly grew another head or something.

"You do know that we play games in other stadiums than our own, right?" Coach asked, his voice gentle. Fatherly again. Kinda. Like if your dad happened to be explaining to you why Fido wasn't coming home anymore.

She frowned. "You do?"

"Hey," Nate interrupted, throwing broken shell onto the coffee table and reaching for another nut to crack. "Free trip to L.A., what other plans do you have?" he spoke with his mouth full. Really full. How many nuts had he taken?

She glanced at the floor around his feet. Wished she hadn't.

She took a breath and opened her mouth to shoot down what she realized was a well thought-out cohesive argument. It was a greater surprise than the trip, so she shrugged and said, "OK." Still, she had the vague sense that she'd just lost an argument to an ape and wasn't sure what to do with that.

"So," Coach took over again, "starting today, you're Nate's girlfriend."

"NO!" Nate and Amanda looked at each other. If the look of surprise on her face was anything like the one on his, Amanda was sure Coach Johnson would be having a good laugh. She looked at the other man. Nope, no humor there at all.

Damn.

"Look, Mr. Johnson," Amanda put out both hands in a pleading gesture. "I know that a job is a job, but I *do* have a reputation to think of. I do need to protect that reputation."

"Wait," Nate dropped his filbert on the table, still intact. It bounced, landing somewhere near Amanda's foot. "Are you saying that going out with me would... *hurt your reputation?*"

"Of course," Amanda said, leaning down to pick up a nut, holding it in her fist. "You sound surprised."

Nate flapped his arms. For a moment Amanda wondered if he were attempting liftoff. "Are you hearing this, Coach?"

Coach Johnson had evidently accomplished what he'd needed to with this little visit. He was already on his feet and halfway to the door. He paused with his hand on the doorknob, turning his body only slightly so that Amanda could see his face.

Seriously, the guy never smiled.

Until now.

"So, airport tomorrow, 6PM. And, Amanda, I should warn you these things get a lot of press coverage, so wear something appropriate." Coach looked her up and down. His gaze pausing on her fuzzy slippers.

"Wait, what?"

"And you!" He turned on Nate. "That means you can't go trolling for women. No ass on this trip. NONE!"

Nate shot to his feet. "Seriously? Coach, come on! I have a friend in L.A. Several, actually. Nothing? How can you ask me to do that?"

Coach Johnson smiled and stepped toward him, clasping a hand on Nate's shoulder. "I can't ask something like that from you, Nate." He smiled bigger as Nate visibly relaxed. "I'm not asking, I'm telling. *No girls at all!* You have a girlfriend now, and you're going to stay faithful to her."

Nate's eyes darted to Amanda and back. They'd taken on a rather panicked look if the amount of white showing was any indicator. "Coach, if I stay celibate I'm not at my best on the field. I can't play worth shit!"

"Nate!" Coach slapped the shoulder a second time. Hard enough to rock the big man slightly. "That's bullshit. And, for the record, you've been benched, remember?"

"What's 'appropriate'?" Amanda asked, completely lost.

"It's what someone would wear that was classy enough to date me!" Nate snapped, his eyes never leaving Coach.

Amanda looked down at her V-neck red pullover and jeans, and wondered what was wrong with what she had on. "What, am I too clean for you? What's it take? Curlers? Bubble gum? NASCAR t-shirts with a gravy stain?" She snorted. "Teddy bear PJs?"

"Enough!" Coach bellowed. "You," he pointed at Nate, "help her. And be nice." He turned without another word and left. The door banged shut behind him with enough force to knock a painting off the wall. The glass shattered on the still-life of two calla lilies.

Nate and Amanda stared at each other. Two pouting children regarding each other, neither about to make a move to clean up the mess.

"No girls." Nate muttered.

"Gee, thanks." Amanda said, crossing her arms. Her eyes narrowed dangerously. "What am I, another guy?"

He eyed her. "Are you saying you want to have sex in L.A.?"

"Not with you," she answered quickly. Maybe too quick.

Not that he noticed.

He put his hand out, grabbing the doorknob. He was positively sneering. "Then, yes, you're one of the guys."

Chapter 6

Amanda shook her head, but kept running on the treadmill. *The star quarterback of a major football team owns a mansion with two guesthouses, a pool, and a gym, but he had to go all the way across town to use the gym at the stadium?*

And, of course, as his newly appointed 'girlfriend', she had to go with him.

Maybe he had to work out at the Broncos' gym. Or maybe he was doing it just to annoy her.

Face it: if he'd been an actual child wouldn't you be doing local errands, taking him along?

She plodded along, considering the fantasy. Savoring it, actually. Picturing playdates with young Nathanial making sandcastles with his little friends, while she would be sitting close by, on a rather ubiquitous park bench, comfortably doing research for her thesis.

Not jogging on a treadmill, which was nothing more than a hyperactive welcome mat with delusions.

But, somehow, and she was still puzzling it out, this bad job was getting worse and worse. Now she was a faux girlfriend, like arm candy to an ape. Ok, maybe 'arm candy' wasn't *entirely* accurate, but it did give her a slight thrill to think of herself that way. 'Ape' though...she stood by that phrasing, considering it to be right on the nose.

So, here she was, in the vast cavern of the Broncos' training room, surrounded by dozens of machines designed to inflict pain and extract sweat, all of them empty but for one idiot and his pretend girlfriend.

She glanced over at him. He looked serene as a Buddha with those damn earbuds shoved all the way in his ears, no doubt trying to keep the last two remaining brain cells from flying out while he ran. He matched her stride for stride for a while and glanced at her from the corner of his eye. He sped up the treadmill to a sort of trot, and she matched it without looking. He bumped up the speed to a slight sprint, and she raised her speed accordingly.

Nate put his machine on a long-legged, ground-loping run. Amanda lowered her stance and stretched her long legs out and ran as fast as she could next to him. He was not going to get the best of her!

The pace wasn't brutal but she was pushing herself. She got comfortable in her stride and looked around again. Seriously, it was a nice gym. A real shame that no one used it. Not that there was anyone else who would be stupid enough to travel all that way...

"HEY, NATE!" a booming voice called from the doorway behind her. Amanda had to grab the rails on the treadmill to stay upright, nearly tripping, and had to jog to catch up. Her heart-rate monitor flared, beeping wildly at the sudden increase.

She let go of the bar before it recorded anything else about her.

"BILLY!" Nate yelled back, and pumped his fist without breaking stride.

The man apparently named Billy walked over to them. He was wearing a sweatshirt with a faded image of the Green Hornet, shorts, and sneakers. He was also something close to the Greek ideal of a god. He was at least 6'5", broad in the shoulders, and appeared to have a large chest hiding under Kato's face.

"Hello," he smiled at her, ignoring Nate completely. "With who do I have the pleasure?" His smile nearly melted her right knee. She even forgave him the bad grammar.

Nate sighed like a child expected to recite a poem. "Billy Bartock, this is Amanda..." He blinked a few times, obviously without the slightest clue as to what her last name was.

"Jones!" Amanda said, giving him a look designed to bring him to his knees.

Nate kept running, facing forward. Totally unaware.

Bastard. Idiot wasn't even winded. Here she barely had the breath to speak, and Nate was loping along smoothly and barely breaking a sweat.

She smiled at Billy, maybe throwing in a few extra kilowatts just to keep things interesting. Besides, he was pretty to look at. "Jones, Amanda Jones. Just Amanda." She even managed a slight purr on the last syllable. Just because she could.

"Coach says Amanda's my new girlfriend," Nate said, looking up at the TV screen across from him. "You see Buffalo's game last night? How'd they pull that out of their asses?" He popped his earbuds back in without waiting for an answer.

Amanda sputtered and shook her head. "He's kidding around. He's just..." she conserved her breath. Why didn't Nate sweat? She could barely see at this point.

"... an ass?" Billy finished helpfully. He shook his head. "Sorry, I shouldn't say that."

"Yes, you should."

"Billy! Nate!"

Nate was too intent on whatever song he was listening to, doubtless sung by a large purple dinosaur, to notice another newcomer. Billy waved at the male voice by the door. "Hey Nick!" He pointed a thumb at Amanda. "Meet Amanda Jones, Nate's girlfriend."

Behind her came a low rumbling reply that melted her hips. Or that might have been the treadmill doing that. A moment later the mysterious Nick came into view. Apparently, the Greek ideals of gods gathered around football players. Amanda realized Nick was *the* Nick Page. Amanda recognized him from the newspaper article wherein Nate was accused of roasting a goat. According to Coach Johnson (she made a mental note to learn the man's first name), Nick was unaware of the luau on his driveway before the fire department arrived.

Or so he said.

Nick was wearing a t-shirt that was easily four or five times too big, and sweat pants. Where Billy was huge and built along the lines of a WWII tank, Nick was built more like a runner. In his case, like a runner who could carry a girl as he ran. Amanda tried to shake that image out of her head. She failed.

"Nice to meet you, Amanda," Nick said, and flashed another winning smile.

Amanda heard herself make a noise like 'hurmmph' and tried to get some air back. If she couldn't make proper speech, she wasn't going to lose the oxygen she needed to breathe. She prayed they would think the red in her face was something less embarrassing, like a stroke.

Billy and Nick walked off to stretch on the mats. They seemed to be talking about her and looking at Nate as they flexed and stretched and pulled and... Amanda lost her footing again and pounded the treadmill hard to keep her feet under her. She got her rhythm back and tried to not look at either man.

Which worked out just fine. For a few minutes, anyway.

Then, as one, their stretches finished, they removed their shirts.

Bare-chested and with a slight sheen of perspiration, they warmed up one more time.

Almost immediately Amanda's right toes hooked over her left ankle and she face-planted on the speeding treadmill. The blasted thing shot her crumpled body backwards like she'd been launched like a torpedo.

Her sweats glided smoothly over the heavily waxed floors and she spun as she slid across the gym. A neatly stacked collection of jump ropes, medicine balls, and juggling pins scattered upon impact, leaving her feeling like she'd just visited the wrong end of a bowling alley.

Amanda looked up into the faces of two gorgeous, bare-chested men. "Oh, shit," she mumbled, swallowing hard so as not to throw up. "I'm okay."

She looked over to where Nate was still driving his long legs on the treadmill. He never looked her way, but she swore if he so much as cracked a smile she'd spend every last dime she had breaking it.

"You alright?" Nick asked. The two men knelt beside her.

She giggled, the laughter taking on a hysterical note that ended on a sob. Then she just looked for a hole in the wall to crawl into until this was all over.

Nate's rhythmic *stomp, stomp* on the treadmill continued as Billy picked her up and carried her to a bench.

Amazing.

It really was possible to be deeply in lust while feeling like you'd been hit by a bus.

Chapter 7

Nothing about this job seemed to be easy.

She stood now, utterly lost.

It wasn't like she'd never been to the airport in Denver before. She'd been past that devil horse enough times that it didn't at least stop her heart as she drove into the terminal on Friday night.

Much. Let's face it, the damned thing with the glowing red eyes was creepy as hell, especially at night. Whatever had possessed the powers that be to plant such a thing at the entrance to the airport was beyond her. Especially since it had killed its own creator.

For that matter, it was probably scoping out the incoming cars looking for its next victim.

She shuddered and drove around to the parking lot, fighting traffic which seemed heavier than normal. Of course, people tended to fly places on Friday nights so she wound up way out in the boondocks, making her feet an absolute misery as she crossed the parking lot. And crossed the parking lot. And crossed another parking lot. Then stood forever looking for information on the big board about her flight out to L.A.

I should've taken Nate up on his offer to drive in with him.

No. I should've just stayed home.

The problem was, nothing looked right on the board. United had flights to L.A. but nothing that left at 8:00 pm exactly. With a sigh, she headed for the ticket counter, walking past strange murals that did nothing for her mood, leaving her more creeped out than ever.

The Denver airport was just...weird.

Kind of like her job.

Kind of like her fake boyfriend.

The girl at the counter gave her a blank look when she asked about the flight. She appeared to be about sixteen years old, peering through Harry Potter glasses at her computer terminal as if the magic words would appear. Or maybe she was willing the information to scroll across the screen.

"It might help to hit some keys," Amanda finally said helpfully.

This earned a glare and a warning glance from the woman working at the terminal next to them.

"The Broncos have their own chartered flight through United," the woman said, looking Amanda up and down and oozing false politeness. "They certainly do not take unauthorized passengers."

Eyes met.

The woman was steel. Unyielding. It didn't help that the chirpy 15-year-old was smirking. Amanda leveled her with a look that should have left her shaking. "If you want to be taken seriously, lose the ponytails," she said, knowing it was petty, and stalked away from the desk before they could call security.

Or hopefully before they would call security.

She fought the urge to break into a run as she moved past the freaky murals again, moving into the main part of the terminal. The place was cavernous, big open floor space in the middle taken up by security checkpoints, and shops and restaurants all around the edges. The ceiling towered over her in peaks, giving the whole place the look of a demented circus tent.

There were no signs anywhere to give her even the remotest clue where chartered flights would be. Or how she would go about finding them.

It's all Nate's fault, she thought viciously as she whipped out her cell phone. Not that she had any idea how exactly it was Nate's fault. Only that it was.

Obviously.

She brought up his contact and had only just dialed when she heard a commotion behind her. Of course she heard a commotion behind her. What else could it be but...

"TNT!"

The name went up from a hundred voices at least, causing business travelers to pause in their driven powerwalks, and for mothers to pull teenage daughters in close, as if to somehow shield them from unspeakable horror.

Amanda closed her eyes and counted to ten.

And made it as far as four before a big meaty hand closed around her upper arm and her entire body was shifted abruptly to the left as he simply started to tow her away. "What're you doing way out here? Coach is having a fit. The plane's loaded and ready to go. It's almost eight."

Being pulled through the airport with her eyes closed—not such a good idea. Opening them when she could already feel the press of the crowds and the continuing shouts and chants erupting around them seemed even worse. Still, she opened them just as they shot through a doorway into an area she'd never seen before. Some uniformed guard was waving them through, and it was all she could to do hang on to her carryon as he rushed her down a long hallway that came out...somewhere.

Somewhere outside as it turned out.

A plane stood on the tarmac, engines already at a high whine.

They weren't as late as she'd supposed. There were still players milling about and the last of the luggage was just being shunted aboard.

"I thought you said they were ready to go," she muttered through clenched teeth, shaking his hand off and bending to rub her ankle which had somehow been kicked in the mad rush.

"Miss Jones, I thought I told you to dress appropriately!"

Coach Johnson didn't sound happy. In fact, he sounded downright angry. In slow motion, Amanda straightened and turned, noting that every player on the team and no small amount of ground crew were all staring at her.

Amanda looked down at her denim jacket and white silk cami, unable to see anything wrong. Her gaze dropped to the black leather micro-mini skirt. The stockings and impossibly high heels.

Then her eyes went to the coach, who stood a short distance away, his face red enough to clash with the blue and orange of his Broncos jacket.

The team stood in eerie silence behind him.

"What? You told me to dress the way someone who dated him would..."

With that she adjusted the strap of her carryon and pushed right past Nate and the coach, nothing with a certain degree of pleasure that Nate seemed about as dumbstruck as everyone else, as if he'd only just noticed her clothing.

She even managed to push through the line of gaping football players and make it all the way up the stairs that led into the aircraft.

Her exit was absolutely perfect, she noted with a grin. She left them all with their mouths gaping. She tilted her chin just a little higher, straightened her shoulders...and BAM!

Falling flat on her face at the doorway to the aircraft when her heel caught on a seam in the metal there wasn't exactly the exit she had hoped for.

She wound up with her face buried in the carpet, ass in the air, and thinking that wearing the bright red thong to complete the outfit hadn't been the best idea after all.

Chapter 8

"Wow!" George let out a long, low whistle as they sat down in the stadium. Amanda had managed to make it through the flight and limo to the stadium with her body intact. Her dignity, not so much. "These are prime seats! How much did this cost you?" George whistled again.

"Actually," Amanda said, squaring her shoulders a bit and allowing more than a hint of smugness out in her smile and her tone, "they were a gift, so you can just relax and enjoy the game."

"We're on the 50-yard line in the front row!" George was back on his feet, peering down the field and then turning to look at how many rows of seats were piled behind him. "There's no way NOT to enjoy it!"

Amanda laughed and pulled on his arm, trying to bring him back down to earth. "Well, you're the only one in the entire family who actually cares about football, so I thought of you. Besides, who else do I know in L.A.?"

"Yeah, and you're the sister I never had, too." He grinned, and flagged down a guy selling who-knows-what.

"Oh, come on!" Amanda had to shout to be heard over the crowd. Was it just her or were they getting louder? "We practically grew up together! And it's not just because you're my only cousin, either. I'm sure that...since when do you drink soda?"

"Soda?" George blinked and looked at the plastic cup he'd just gotten for a minute before passing it over to her. "You drink it. I just wanted the commemorative cup. Be sure to give it to me when you're done."

She opened her mouth to protest but George was already on his feet, screaming with the rest of the losers...er... fans. The Broncos football team was filing out onto the field from the... place-under-the-stands-that-they-were-in-whatever-it's-called.

She stood, albeit reluctantly, taking a sip of overly-sweet soda and almost choking when it turned out to be cherry cola. The players came storming out onto the field and ran up along the side. She recognized Billy, who caught her eye. He nudged Nick and they trotted over to where she stood at the railing.

"Hey, Amanda!" Billy called out, all grins and pre-game testosterone. "Nice to see you again!"

"You're looking like you're doing better!" Nick added, nudging Billy who went off into whoops of laughter.

Amanda colored and waved. "Thanks, guys!" After a moment, she laughed with them. It was either that or cry. Besides, they were good enough boys. There was no harm in their teasing and she could be a good sport about things.

That's when she felt a vise bruising her arm and realized that George had a death grip on her bicep. "Oh, George, this is Billy and Nick. Guys, this is George."

"I know. Holy shit! Holy shit...what the hell, Amanda?"

Amanda stared at her cousin for a long moment, waiting for something ... *anything* else, but he seemed to have exhausted his repertoire.

"OK then..." she said, turning back to the players and smiling.

"Hey, enjoy the game!" Billy called as he and Nick ran back to the bench.

Amanda stole a glance at George, who was still waving long after the guys were gone. His eyes had a glassy look that she hadn't seen since Junior Prom when Mary Beth Walker had asked him to dance. She smirked. "I have to say, George, I'm really impressed. You are a silver-tongued devil!"

"Shut up."

At least that's what she thought he'd said. He'd collapsed into his seat as if he were a puppet whose strings had been cut. Between the roar of the crowd and the fact that he was holding his face in his hands, it was impossible to tell. She sat back down next to him.

He let out a long groan. "I made an ass of myself!"

Amanda laughed and patted his arm. "Yeah, you did. Have something to drink." With that she shoved the cup, sorry, COMMEMORATIVE cup, of whatever abomination of cola and fruit into his hands, and watched with a certain amount of glee as he drained it dry without seeming to taste a single drop.

Stifling another laugh, Amanda turned her attention to Nate. He seemed distracted. He'd been sitting on the bench, and was in full uniform as if he expected to play. Yet his focus seemed off, almost uninterested in what was going on as the teams lined up on the field. His whole posture telegraphed an intense longing, and periodically he would jump up and try to talk to one of the coaches. Especially Coach Johnson. Who ignored him completely.

Behind her the stadium erupted into a cacophony of cat calls, booing, and even death threats which all seemed to be part of the enjoyment of the game. Especially the death threats, as they were aimed at the players on both sides, the referees, coaches, and even a cheerleader or two.

Not that it was all negative attention. Periodically some scantily-clad female would scream a marriage proposal across the field to a favorite player. Amanda wondered briefly what would happen if one of the guys out there suddenly turned around and accepted.

Belatedly, Amanda realized that Nate wasn't looking at the field anymore. He was staring at her. Amanda waved brightly and nudged George. "Wave to Nate, aka T.N.T.," she said, hoping to restore his damaged pride. George waved, but it was a sad little thing, halfhearted. He would take some time to get over this embarrassment.

Thankfully he loosened up somewhat as the game progressed. Beer helped. By the end of the first quarter George had his shirt off and was twirling it over his head as he cheered, slapping high fives with those seated around them as if they were all part of some huge extended family. Some huge extended and very close family. There were a lot of fist bumps and howls as their team scored. That the guys were rooting against Nate and his buddies didn't bother Amanda in the least. The whole thing was absolutely outlandish, especially as she had no clue what it meant when the guys ran up and down the field and just where the points were all coming from.

Which didn't even begin to address her disappointment when she'd initially found out a quarter was all of fifteen minutes. Her vision of the game being over in an hour ground to a halt as the clock did. Honestly, the timer was at a standstill more often than being in motion. At this rate the game would take all day.

Still, there was a certain amount of fun in watching. Somewhere around the second quarter, Amanda finally got George to put his shirt back on and even convinced him that taking the time to explain the game to her might someday result in further tickets to games. So, heads together, he pointed and gestured, his mouth close to her ear so she could hear him over the noise.

She thought she was learning something, until a nudge from the guy seated next to her brought her head up and showed her an entire new aspect to the game of football that she'd never imagined.

Following the pointing hands of the helpful attendees around her, Amanda looked up and saw herself...and her cousin on the huge screen that dominated the skyline. The two of them were framed with a gigantic heart and the words "KISSING CAM" flashed over their faces.

The fans were going crazy, screaming, "KISS HER! KISS HER!" Amanda nudged George, who looked up, leaving his jaw somewhere down around his chest. He looked at her and shrugged, as if asking her what to do next. Amanda shrugged back and kissed his cheek, much to the rather vocal disappointment of the crowd.

She hunkered back down in her seat and looked for Nate. He was gone. She'd missed his exit. For all she knew he was making a run to the bathroom, or more likely off to grab some beer now that the realization that he wasn't playing after all had sunk in.

After a half hour, she decided he wasn't returning.

She swore under her breath. Her charge ran off and had a good thirty-minute head-start on her while she'd waffled back and forth over whether she should have gone looking for him or not. She jumped up and ran to the rail and yelled "BILLY! NICK!" Her voice was one of many screaming out players' names. A security guard spotted her and began to thread his way through the crowd to her.

She jumped and waved her arms. When the big screen caught her again, it wasn't a Kissing Cam. This time it was showing a rather exuberant fan—a young girl bouncing up and down... all over. She squealed and covered herself. But at least Billy saw the screen from where he was standing on the sidelines, shaking off the effects of a particularly nasty tackle.

"Hey, Amanda, what's wrong?" he yelled as he trotted up to her.

"Where's Nate?"

Billy shrugged and waved off the guard. "She's with me!" Suddenly the large monitor was on her again. The guard hesitated and slowly withdrew, looking like he was ready to rush Amanda if the 110-lb. girl decided to injure the 350-lb. football player.

Billy turned and caught Nick's eye. He pointed to Amanda and then to the bench. Nick rubbed his armpits and made a walking motion with his fingers.

"He hit the showers and left," Billy translated.

Amanda smacked the railing and kicked the post holding it up, though it mashed her toes in the pretty, decorative boots she was wearing. Billy shrugged, smiled, and trotted back to the bench. She scurried back to her seat, groping underneath, trying to find her purse. "George! I'm sorry, can you find your own way home? I have to go... work."

George looked at her for a long moment. "I drove."

"I know...." She pursed her lips, realizing that this conversation would have gone a whole lot better a couple of beers ago. "Can I borrow your car?"

"What?" George blinked a few times. "Wait... what?" He was obviously still trying to catch up.

"Here," Amanda reached into her purse and pulled out a plastic badge Coach Johnson—*what the hell was his first name?!*—gave her. "You can use this to get into the locker room, or so I'm told."

Somehow this penetrated the alcohol-induced fog. George took the badge reverently, looking at it the way Harrison Ford looked at the idol in the opening of *Raiders of the Lost Ark*. He reached into his pocket and fished out the keys without looking. "Keep the car," he said, his voice sounding a little strangled. "I don't need it."

Amanda didn't give him time to re-think it. She ran up the steps and out the exit. She was pleased with herself that she only got lost once, but it took asking three people for directions before she found one who spoke English. By the time she got to George's car, Nate had at least a forty-five-minute head-start.

She finally managed to thread her way through the parking lot and paused at the road. It occurred to her then that she had no idea which way she ought to be going. Los Angeles was beyond huge. Did he even have usual haunts out here? She thought to call the coach, but it was obvious even to her that he was busy.

Amanda pulled the car over to the side of the road, leaving it idling while she thought this through. Terrific. Nate could be anywhere right now, and she was probably unemployed and didn't even know it. Tomorrow she could read all about where Nate was, as it would be in all the papers. All she needed was a time machine...

She caught herself. Maybe it didn't need to be that complicated.

A quick search on her phone brought up a recent article on the best sports bars in the city. Thankfully it came with a description of each of the places. Most were too cutesy for what she was looking for, but a handful came up with the words that would appeal to a football superstar who fed off adulation and free beer.

"Party" and "Excitement" for example. Mentions of wings were a bonus.

Armed with information and not much time, Amanda got a crash course in driving in L.A. while thanking all the gods at whichever computer company had created the GPS app on her phone.

It took nearly an hour and three bars before she found his rental car in a parking lot. Thankfully she'd been around to hear the argument he'd had with coach when he'd informed everyone that he'd rented the thing and wouldn't be needing a ride to the stadium on the team bus. It helped that he'd been bragging about being able to score that particular model of sports car at the time.

The 'bar' in question had turned out to be more of a dive than the article had led on, complete with neon women posing over beer bottles and the rusty twang of country music blaring loud enough to be heard from the sidewalk.

Nate was at a table in the corner with a tall glass, staring at his reflection in the surface of the table. Surprisingly, though the bar was crowded, everyone was leaving him alone.

"There you are!" Amanda slid into the seat opposite him, earning more than one sympathetic look from the nearby patrons, which kind of made her wonder what had been happening in the last couple of hours since he'd escaped. Other than the end of the game. The screens every few feet along the walls were playing a highlight reel, which seemed to include an awful lot of footage of her...bouncing up and down.

Nate looked up, swore, and rolled his eyes so far back he could have seen the back of his head.

Seriously? He was going to become a petulant toddler now? She slammed her hands down on the table between them, hard enough to make several bottles rattle. The hot sauce tipped over. "Do you not want to play anymore? Are you looking to stay on the bench?"

"What the hell are you talking about?" Nate looked up at her, frowning with what she would swear looked an awful lot like genuine confusion.

"THAT!" She pointed at the glass on the table.

"Ginger ale?"

Amanda stared at the glass, looked back up him, then back to the glass again. Finally she reached over and picked it up gingerly, taking a cautious sip.

Ginger ale.

"Uh...."

Nate stood but made no move to leave the table, instead towering over her. "You are wound up tighter than my grandfather's watch," he growled. "I'm sorry if I dragged you away from the game, but we're supposed to be carrying on some damn illusion here and I'm keeping up my part of the bargain."

"What?"

"We're not supposed to be seeing others, *remember*?"

"Wait. What? Oh, shit. That's my—"

"And here you are on the Kissing Cam? Any idea how that makes me look? Not only am I benched, but the girl I'm supposed to be dating is on the kissing cam with some scarecrow-looking guy..."

It was Amanda's turn to stand up. It would have been a lot more impressive if she were taller. "Hold on a min—"

"And then you bust in here like you're pulling a kid out of a forest fire?! Lady, I might be a screw-up, but I'm still a man!"

"You're—"

"You know what?" Nate said and took Amanda's arm. "You're coming with me; it's time you shoved a crowbar into that tight little crevice where you keep your soul and let some light in."

"Would you please—"

Nate was already out the door and Amanda was pulled along in his wake. She saw the bartender shake his head sadly as the door slammed shut behind them. Across the street was a small car, the driver of which was taking pictures.

Oh, that can't be good.

"What do you think you're doing?" she asked Nate, a hint of panic in her voice as she planted her heels in the sidewalk and refused to be moved.

Not that it mattered.

"I'm retiring." He hauled her across the parking lot and opened a car door. Not to her car, to his. The Ferrari. "And I'm going out in style."

Amanda sat heavily and barely noticed when he lifted her legs to wedge her into the car and closed the door.

"Oh, I am so gonna get fired," she said to the car, since no one else seemed to be listening.

Chapter 9

Amanda couldn't help but be astounded.

Nate was a thousand miles from home, in the afternoon, his entire team was probably just leaving the field, and yet he drove unerringly to a wild party. Beach house, surf, noise, private gate—a whole stereotypical L.A. blowout.

"How the hell did you know about this place?" she asked as he slipped through the gate. He'd given his name and the gate spread open for him like... well, Amanda didn't want to continue with that particular analogy. Jennifer had been a friend once.

"I get out and meet people!" Nate shouted over the rap he'd been playing since they'd left the bar. "You should try it!" He grinned like a kid at Christmas, and pulled up the long drive to a mansion that squatted like an anti-lighthouse. Instead of keeping ships safe from rocks, it lured football players to their doom. And to the end of their careers.

"You can't just... quit," Amanda said for the umpteenth time since they'd gotten in the car. Only, this time he answered. It was an interesting novelty.

"Actually, I can," Nate said as he pulled up between an Audi and a Toyota. Amanda ignored that for the moment. "I took Coach's advice, and read my contract." He got out of the car and waited while she extracted herself from the undersized car. She thought that, from his perspective, it must have been like watching a birthing video. "It says that I can 'retire' anytime I want to, so long as I don't play for anyone else and that I return a couple of million. I don't even care anymore." He tossed something to her in a long arc that ended in her palm. All she had to do was close her hand. She still managed to drop it.

"You're giving me your car?" she asked, looking at the keys at her feet.

"Don't be an idiot." He laughed, and ruffled her hair like she was a little kid. "I'm designating you. I'm getting drunk." He turned and shouted something like "LEON" in the general direction of the house, but it was so guttural she couldn't be sure. An answering cry from the front porch did at least confirm that the frat boy was in season again. She had to jog to catch up to him.

She'd left the hotel expecting to hook up with a long-lost cousin, watch a football game, and regain some of the dignity that she'd lost getting on the plane. Going to a party had not been on the agenda. Looking at the other guests, the outfit she'd worn to the airport would have been much more appropriate than the shorts and team t-shirt she wore right now. She felt positively dowdy.

She opened the door to the house and was almost blasted back off the porch. The music was so blaring that the beat of the drums pressed against her chest and slammed into her sinus cavity. Amanda's entire body vibrated to the thrumming. From where she stood, she could see a large table in the middle of the room that sagged under the weight of the food and booze piled haphazardly on it. Paper plates cozied up to cut glass and what looked to be an actual Rembrandt sketch. Most of the partiers wore swimwear, or dental floss pretending to be swimwear. The women wore even less.

Amanda caught a glimpse of Nate; his shirt was already off and he was greeting a throng of pretty young women who lingered too long with each hug. Amanda found her way to the back door, seeking asylum from the sound and skin. She found herself facing the Pacific Ocean for the first time in her life. She was stunned and stood framed in the back door, just staring into the vast eternity of the magnificent sight.

"I SAID EXCUSE ME!" a voice behind her said and she felt a tap on her back. She got out of the way of traffic, in this case a barely-dressed young woman who padded out the door and down to the beach.

Amanda looked around, grabbed a bottle, slipped out of her sneakers and socks, and followed.

The sunset over the ocean was everything everyone ever said it was, creating a slow explosion of color and cloud and light and shadow. It flared and faded all at once over the great expanse of water until the surf was nothing more than a great nothingness that swept over the beach back and forth, whispering as each wave spent itself on the sand. She sat watching it, enjoying her drink and the moment.

"There you are."

She turned and looked up at Nate. He was still bare-chested, but was holding out his shirt for her. "You looked cold."

"A little," she admitted, her voice almost a whisper. This beach, this moment, was too beautiful for confrontations. "I'm surprised how quickly it cools off here."

She said nothing as he wrapped his shirt around her shoulders, but it felt... comfortable, even safe. She grasped it and held it closed around her arms. "Aren't you going to get cold?"

"Eventually. But not yet." He smiled at her and for a moment she saw it, that utterly charming dimple, that way his eyes softened and caressed. It was for this that every woman in the country fell at his feet. Who wouldn't want to be on the receiving end of a look like that?

She swallowed hard. Suddenly unsure. "Aren't you missing the party?"

"The party is missing me." Nate smiled again, and looked at her carefully. "You're drunk." It wasn't a question.

Amanda colored and looked down at her bare feet. She nodded. "I think so."

"How many of those did you have?" Nate asked, pointing at the bottle of beer in her hand.

"Almost finished it," Amanda said proudly. "The whole thing."

"You got drunk on a single bottle?" Nate took a step back.

"Is that bad?" Amanda asked, looking up at him. Damn, it was a long way to look up and up and up. She got a little dizzy. She threw out a hand to stabilize herself and it landed on his chest. His thick, muscular chest. The warm skin felt good against her palm, and she held it there for a long moment, thinking how small and delicate it seemed. She leaned in and kissed his chest. It felt warm on her lips, too. And on her forehead. And her cheek.

She didn't remember putting her arms around him and couldn't imagine what happened to the empty beer bottle, but he felt so... warm. That was the word—warm. She turned her head so her chin sat on his chest and she looked up to where the two of his faces were wobbling in front of her.

"How come... how come you're not drunk?" she asked him. It was almost an accusation.

He chuckled. "I kinda am."

"How many bottles did you have?" she asked, pushing herself away from him and turning in a slow pirouette. The music from the house was faint, the surf creating a better melody for dancing.

"Of what?"

"Beer!" Amanda stopped and threw her hand out to wave the bottle at him, but she couldn't find it. In fact, her hand was empty. She stared at it a long moment, as if staring long enough might bring it back somehow. Oddly enough it didn't. She snorted, the whole thing suddenly very funny. "I bet you had more than one!"

"Twelve," he said, counting it out on his fingers for her, then giving up as he ran out of fingers. "And half a bottle of scotch. And some gin."

She pulled back from him. "Hilly shot!" She licked her lips. That didn't sound right somehow. "Holly shite!" She gave up. "That's a lot!"

"I've been in training a long time!" he said and lunged forward to catch his shirt. He missed and it slid off her shoulders, pooling in the soft sand. She reached her hand up to his neck and hung there for a moment, letting her hands explore the thick muscles of his back. She discovered her toes were flexing and she was rising, closer and closer to him. His chest had been interesting, but it was nothing compared to his steel jaw, square and framed with just a little stubble. Those eyes that penetrated hers.

Her lips covered his and his hands, the large, strong, so capable hands ran up and down her back, finally taking her derrière in his huge palms and pulling her up to his lips, kissing her deeply and fully. His hands massaged her buttocks, pulling them into his massive grip as his tongue found hers.

She ran her hands down the broad expanse of his back, running her fingers through his rough hair. She barely took a break from him long enough to slip off her shirt and toss it uncaring beside the other.

She worked her way down his neck with her lips and fumbled for his belt. She was filled with a sudden need, a burning basic 'must have' like air or water or food. She slapped her own belly, trying to tear off his belt and open his pants, but when she finally succeeded the sight of him made her gasp.

He was thick, so thick and long. He woke to her touch, lifting in the darkness to her, and without giving herself time to think about it she fell to her knees and pulled him into her throat, loving the way he filled her. She grabbed his ass and slowly, so slowly, lowered her head onto him and swallowed, easing him down her throat.

She took a deep breath and allowed him to close off her airway. She sucked and licked and bit and massaged his gorgeous shaft all while stroking his skin. Her mind had kicked out completely somewhere along the way. For once there was no nagging little voice about jobs and responsibility. There was only him. Only here. Here and now as she bounced her head against him, swallowing his full length and letting it slide back along her tongue and over her teeth. She delighted in his taste, in the way he felt in her mouth, in her throat, as she pulled back and sucked the head while flicking the tip of him with her tongue.

He pulled away suddenly; she thought she'd done something wrong, but he laid her out over the shirt she'd dropped in the sand and pulled off her shorts and underwear savagely, as though his need was as bad as hers.

She was whimpering, pulling at him with a frantic urgency as he parted her thighs and dropped his head between her legs, his tongue flashing and flickering over her. It was electric, as though all the sensations of her body were concentrated in the single point of her clit. It ran through her, springing every nerve ending; every breath was caught and held and her throat burned from stifling the screams that would bring the entire party down on them as he probed her depths and grasped the little bud with his teeth. She whimpered and begged, though she had no idea what she was begging for as he used his thumbs to spread her folds. The air was cold against her heated center and she gasped, thinking that she would lose it here and now, and she wasn't ready for that, not by a long shot. She wanted more...

As though reading her mind, he moved his head again, diving back into her sex like a man starved, flashing tongue and magic fingers, bringing her to the edge of orgasm again and again, but pulling back until she was weeping with frustration.

Then she felt him shift and she gasped and bit her lip as he rose above her, his entire body outlined dimly against the darkening sky as he entered her, piercing her to the core, stretching her, opening her to take his length. He slipped into her wetness easily. She was ready to surrender to him. More than ready. She sighed as he filled her. It was like coming home.

But even this was only the beginning. He slipped between her folds, moving his hips against her, his hardness reaching through her and pressing her from inside out until she thought he would pin her to the soft sand. He filled her and, with her head thrown back in wild abandon, she wrapped her legs around his waist and reveled in the oldest of night-time pursuits. She moved with him, her own hips rising and falling as she pulled herself around him, pulled him into her, until she was well and truly filled. And even then, she wanted more.

Maybe he understood. He took her with a wildness, animalistic almost in the way he pounded into her, until his movements echoed the crashing of the waves on the shore. She met him, frantic for him, kissing every inch of skin. Biting him along the neck and shoulder, tasting his sweat upon her lips and tongue and reveling that he would be so...so...male. So *him*.

When the orgasm came, it wasn't a slow gentle thing like fumbling with boys when she was younger, or the quick, efficient way she pleased herself. She came around him with him buried into her, her legs twitching and jumping, her hips high and back arched, clutching desperately at his body, her fingernails digging into his shoulders, holding her anchored there.

She bent and screamed and bit into his shoulder to keep from crying out worse, to keep from drowning out the vast ocean and its might with her climax. He finished while her body was still spasming and flailing.

Then he collapsed beside her, breathing heavily as if he'd just run the length of the field and scored whatever it was they scored when they ran the length of the field. Words weren't important anymore. Nothing was. She melted into the sand, his massive body curled around her, one giant arm across her breasts in a possessive gesture.

There was nothing to say, so they lay there in silence. Her hand reached. Found his as she thought how odd it was to be lost like this on some unknown beach, in the darkness, next to him, until finally the darkness and the liquor and the languor claimed her.

Chapter 10

Dawn came and Amanda woke stiff, feeling gritty. She opened her eyes and closed them again quickly against the glare of the sun.

Oh shit.

The memories of the night came flooding back to her. She didn't dare turn around behind her, just in case...oh yeah, there was a hand on her thigh.

Shit.

She was naked on a beach, out in the open where anyone could see.

Shit.

She turned, just a little. Yep. It was Nate. Holy mother of.... he was naked, too.

OH SHIT!

Amanda slid out from under his hand, holding it to prevent it from falling and waking him. She edged out from the hole she'd made with her body and tried to hold on to her head before it fell off and rolled down the beach somewhere. Not literally, but it felt like it. Not an easy task given the wave of pain flooding through her.

She fished for her shirt and denim shorts, couldn't find her bra or panties, and after a frantic search remembered that her sneakers were on the porch where she'd left them the night before.

Mostly dressed, she felt a jabbing pain somewhere near the back pocket of the shorts and fished out Nate's keys. For a moment, she considered just taking the car and running but then thought better of it. She spotted his pants crumpled up underneath him and very slowly tucked the car keys into his pocket where he would be sure to find them, and took off over the warming sand to the house. Grabbing her shoes, she found her phone in her hip pocket and called a taxi to get back to the hotel before she could think better of it and instead just book a flight to Timbuktu. Or something.

Please let him be too drunk to remember. She repeated it like a mantra. *Please let him be too drunk to remember.*

The problem was that Amanda remembered. She remembered every detail, every nuance, every feeling. She pushed it down but it refused to stay there, her body screaming from the loss of him.

Thankfully the cab arrived before anyone else surfaced. The ride all the way back to the hotel gave her way too much time to think. It didn't help that the cab driver kept smirking at her in the mirror, as if everything she'd done last night was written all over her face.

At the hotel she paid him, stiffing him the tip because he'd leered at her one too many times. Feeling filthy, and certainly not herself, she slunk to her hotel room without meeting anyone. In minutes she was stripped and under the hot water, where she tried to scald off the memory of last night.

It didn't work.

Still, she stayed put until the water ran cold. She spent most of that time pulling grains of sand out of her hair and from her toes and inventing new names to call Nate. None of them pleasant. Still it was only fair, given the names she was calling herself.

Eventually she fled the shower and curled up in a tiny heap, seated on the bed and wrapped in a hotel robe, rocking back and forth and debating whether she should just look for a job out in L.A. since she was already here.

The knock on her door made her cry out and dive for the blankets.

The problem was she wasn't four, the bogeyman sounded an awful lot like Coach Johnson, and as it turned out he wasn't going to go away until she answered.

Shit.

Her creative range of vocabulary had definitely taken a turn for the worse.

Amanda dragged herself from the bed, wrapping the blanket around herself over the robe, using the layers of fabric as armor.

It was Coach Johnson all right. It was a very angry Coach Johnson. He shoved his way through the door the moment she cracked it. "I said that you were imitating boyfriend-girlfriend," he said without preamble.

Amanda contemplated the floor, wondering what it would take for it to open up and swallow her. They had earthquakes here, didn't they? She sighed, wet her lips and tried to talk, then had to try again when the first attempt didn't work out with anything audible. "I know, I went too far..."

"I *said* not to hook up with anyone out here!" Coach was getting a full head of steam now.

"I didn't think it was going to happen either..."

"I said it to *him*! I didn't think I would have to say it to you! You were the sensible one! You were the one I thought I could trust to understand what's at stake, You, I thought, would be smart enough not to throw away everything for a date!"

Amanda blinked. "I'm not sure what we're talking about right now—"

"You brought a DATE to the game! You were on the KISSING CAM! What the hell?!"

Realization dawned. The blanket drooped. "Are you talking about my cousin, George?"

Coach stared at her. "Cousin? That guy's your cousin?"

Amanda stared at him. "What do you think, that I'd bring a date to my job where I'm supposed to be dating some notorious football player?" She shook her head. "George is a huge football fan. I was using him to explain the game to me and, yeah, have someone to sit with in the stands. As far as the KISSING CAM is concerned, may I point out that it was a kiss on the cheek, for which we were booed?"

Coach actually backed toward the door, glancing over his shoulder as his hand fumbled for the knob. "Well, it's gonna be awkward explaining that to the press, but it should be easily proven..."

"Don't worry about them," Amanda said, flopping into the chair next to the window. "If that's all you wanted, you may as well leave now. The secret is safe. In fact...there was someone with a camera when I left the bar *with Nate*. They probably followed us..." The blood drained from her face. It was a good thing she was sitting down. "Oh. Shit." She looked at Coach with widened eyes. "Could they have... do their cameras see in the dark... Double shit."

Coach stalled out in the act of leaving, letting go of the doorknob and watching the door he'd just opened swing shut under its own steam. When he turned, it was in slow motion. "What are you talking about?"

"Last night. We were on a beach..."

Coach wasn't getting it.

"All night..."

Still not getting it.

"ALL. NIGHT."

Coach got it.

His jaw worked. It took a while for the explosion to build. Amanda pulled the blanket up again, this time not stopping at her shoulders.

"Are you...? You were only supposed to *pretend* to be his girlfriend!"

She peered out from under her fabric tent. "I know! But he was so sad and kept talking about quitting and that was such a ..."

"QUITTING?! No one wants him to quit! What did you do?"

"Me?" Amanda squeaked despite herself, letting the blanket drop back down over her head. "I didn't do anything. He was just under so much pressure and so overwrought..."

She never even heard him move. One minute the blanket was wrapped securely around her, a nice safe little cocoon, the next she'd been tumbled onto the floor, blanket long gone and her robe half off.

"You thought it would be good for him to quit?"

She scrambled to right herself, tugging at the robe to save her modesty, such as it was at this point. "It wasn't my idea!"

"It had to have been... Nate doesn't HAVE ideas of his own!"

That did it.

Amanda was on her feet in an instant, to hell with the robe. "Wait right there! Nate isn't an idiot. You keep treating him like a child and he becomes a child. He's smart, smarter than he lets on. You keep saying these horrible things about him, and you're no better than all the people who want to see him fail! Maybe he should retire, just to get away from people like you! It's bad enough to have a world full of people who want to see him screw up, but at least none of them pretended to have his best interests at heart first!"

"You have his best interests at heart? Really? You're his babysitter. Just because you fucked him doesn't make you any different from a host of women who..."

Amanda's hand left four distinctive red welts across his face.

"Holy shit," Coach said quietly. "You're in love."

Amanda stared at him for a long moment. Then she slapped him again.

Only this time she couldn't hold the stare and fell against him, her fists curling up in the team jacket he habitually wore.

"NO! Please, no. I can't, not now, not with him, especially not with him." Whimpers turned to sobs. The nasty messy kind that left her moaning, with great torrents of tears and snot.

She wasn't a pretty sight when she cried. Never had been. And for once she didn't care.

Coach Johnson held her awkwardly, then after a moment patted her back like her father would have. A new father maybe. One who didn't interact with the kids much.

"I can't fall for Nate... I can't!"

"Too late," Coach said with a sigh that she couldn't help but feel. "Now you have to figure out what you're going to do about it."

"I need to ask you something," Amanda pulled away and looked up into the older man's eyes. They were kindly at the center, but she knew that he could be as immovable as iron.

"Alright." His tone was cautious.

"Do you have a first name?"

He smiled. "Coach," he said and kissed her forehead. He fumbled in his pocket and came up with a somewhat rumpled handkerchief. "It's clean, don't worry." He chucked her under the chin. "Just, work it out before we get back to Denver. I assume Nate's in his room?"

Amanda paused in the act of blowing her nose. "Most... likely..."

There was a long silence while Coach's face went through several shades of red, ending finally in purple. "You lost him? In L.A.? Do you know what kind of damage he can do here?"

She edged backward, her eye on the discarded blanket, thinking it was time to hide again. "He won't."

"Why? Because he slept with you? Because he's quitting anyway? Because he's been benched? Which of these reasons are you expecting to make him completely change his personality?"

Ouch. Point taken. "I..." Amanda dropped her head into her palm. "It was... and he was all..."

With great effort, Coach dropped his voice down to more manageable tones. It was a wonder that hotel security hadn't shown up yet. "Do you remember where you left him at least?"

Amanda nodded.

"I think you've been nearly naked long enough; why don't you put something on and we'll go looking for him?"

"Right!" Amanda said, abandoning the blanket idea. "Good idea... yeah. Only..." She kind of gestured at the door. Her room was small; she could hardly get dressed in front of him.

Not that he hadn't already seen most of it...

She hitched up her robe as Coach turned red for different reasons and walked out of the door with an ominous warning that she had better not waste any time.

She barely took time to breathe. Amanda threw together a sensible outfit, one of the billowing shirts that kept her figure a mystery and a fresh pair of jeans. It was nice to wear something that didn't leave a trail of sand in her wake.

She burst from the room fully dressed, and literally ran into Coach Johnson standing right outside her door. He hadn't been kidding around. She grabbed his arm to keep from falling.

"We got lucky," Coach said, pocketing his cell phone. "I mean besides you getting lucky, *we* dodged a bullet. Nate's back, he was just downstairs returning the rental car and he's in his room now, showering for the trip home."

Coach turned to head back toward the elevators and said over his shoulder, "We are leaving here in two hours. I assume that the outfit you wore on the way here is properly disposed of?"

"Yes..." Amanda said quietly, not even wanting to revisit that particular memory. The entire plane ride to L.A. was something she hoped to never hear about again.

"Maybe you can find something between librarian and hooker in two hours?" The elevator opened and Coach stepped through, leaving Amanda standing in the hallway with the absolute certainty that she had left her room key on the other side of her door. "And your cousin's been calling. He wants his car back."

"So not fair..." She turned and tried her door. Definitely locked. Sighing, she made her way to the reception desk.

Chapter 11

The flight back didn't look like it was going to be any easier than the trip out. She kept her head down as she boarded, and glanced around for a seat. They hadn't been assigned so it left her trying to choose who to sit with. Thankfully, she wasn't the only woman on board. Some of the other players had wives, girlfriends, and significant others on board. Except the women were already sitting together, whispering, laughing quietly at some inside joke only they knew. Even when they weren't together, they were still *together*.

Amanda edged past the single guys who hooted or whistled, and reminded her at the top of their lungs about her last trip, or more specifically that they were speculating about her undergarments on this trip. There was no place for her with the happy couples, and Coach Johnson certainly wasn't her first choice for seat partner. It was embarrassing. She'd been an idiot to think dressing like Nate's choice of woman on the flight here was a smart idea.

Exhausted physically and mentally, she finally elected to sit in a row by herself, where she could lick her wounds in peace and wonder whether she was going to ever live down the infamous fall getting on the plane.

The whole thing was... horribly awkward.

She watched Nate come on board, holding her breath as he walked past, barely sparing her a glance. The fact that she'd dropped her tote bag on the empty seat next to her might have had something to do with it, but truth be told she was a coward and it was the easy way out, right?

She followed his progress with a casual turn of the head, waiting to see what happened as he passed Coach a couple rows back. She half expected him to throw his resignation down on Coach's tray table like from some old movie, but he didn't say a word. Hopefully he was still contemplating it?

Amanda twisted back around until she was facing forward. *Yeah, like you really care. Let's face it, you're upset because you don't have the guts to talk him.*

Well, that at least was a normal response, right? Other people got cold feet. Asked for space. Probably half those couples up front had gone through exactly the same thing.

As if. Couples take breaks for what...a few hours? A day or two tops. What sounds better to you? One year? Two? That sounded about right. *You're not even a bloody couple! You slept with the guy, and he probably doesn't even remember it.* She sighed and dug around in her bag for the book she'd thrown in at the last minute but she didn't even open it, rather held it on her lap, fingers trapped between the pages where she'd left her bookmark.

Yeah, you're an idiot. You slept with the client. What a lovely way to earn your keep. She glanced out of the corner of her eye and looked at Coach. She'd taken the time before departure to buy some decent clothing. She'd headed to a local shop and picked a dress she thought one of the player's wives was wearing. And then decided against it because it cost more than two semesters of classes.

She made do with a lower end shop, and although what she was wearing looked ok, it wouldn't survive a cleaning. Or a second wear by her. It itched and chafed. It felt like sandpaper. But Coach had given her a nod, so she guessed she passed muster even if the thing was giving her a rash.

She groaned for the millionth time in the past few hours. She'd slept with the one and only Nate Thomas. Mr. T.N.T. The man she was supposed to keep in line—not contribute to his delinquency. She deserved to wear sandpaper. It was just punishment for her overactive libido. She had woken under his hand, that broad, strong, capable hand. His entire body was lean and hard and... Talking about hard...

She took that thought and set it under her heel and stomped on it. Repeatedly. Something that her grandmother once said to her about being unforgiven for sins we don't feel guilty about ran through her mind. *Yes, that was good! Grandma. Hold on to that image. Nothing squelches sexual arousal like the image of one's grandmother.* What was that old joke about men trying to control their erections? Cold showers and... football. Damn.

Amanda let her head fall back against the seat. She stared up at the ceiling, or more accurately at the baggage compartment overhead. She was being ridiculous; she knew it, Nate probably knew it, Coach assuredly knew it, damn his unassailable logic. Did he really need to point out to her that she was falling Nate? Which wasn't true. Not. At. All.

Damn it! This was getting her nowhere. Besides, Coach was giving her funny looks. Kind of pointed funny looks, the way he kept clearing his throat to get her attention and twitching his head in Nate's direction.

Right. She needed to get up and walk back to the empty seat beside Nate and sit down. Get back to work.

She would do just that. She was a professional, after all. She ...

The plane jumped and fell and lurched again. Turbulence. The *FASTEN SEATBELTS* light blinked on. Too late now. It was a shame, really, but in turbulence there was a safety issue and the light was on, the plane was jumping, and she was a coward.

Having come to that conclusion, Amanda sighed and settled back in her chair and sipped a bottle of water the attendants had brought out along with a big platter of sandwiches. Apparently, football players needed to eat constantly. The trip up had been one long smorgasbord. Between turbulence both inside and outside, eating was the last thing on her agenda.

So she slunk in her seat again, pretending to be interested in a book she was reading upside down. Eventually Coach gave up clearing his throat and nodding. There was a certain power to being a coward. No one expected too much from you.

She turned around to look at the row where Nate was sitting. No one expected too much from a clown either, did they?

A thought hit her suddenly. Nate played the fool because it was easier and guaranteed his success. No one expected him to excel, did they? Amanda chided herself. As 'professional' as she claimed to be, she hadn't been using her training with Nate, just taking him as a fool like everyone else did. Judging him based on what others said.

She ran through last night with clinical detachment. He'd been more himself then, less the clown. He'd been tender and thoughtful and all that while drunk. Was it all an act with him? An act to get out of...what? Hard work? That didn't fit the mold. From what she could see, he was as dedicated to the team as any. He'd been smashed and tackled and had a dozen 300-lb. men slam him to the ground, and still he smiled and played the fool.

What was it he said? "If I don't play, they're going to forget about me!" Vanity? Somehow it didn't gel; there was something she was missing and she wasn't sure what it was. The one thing she did know was that she wasn't going to figure it out separated from him by several rows.

Amanda took a deep breath and stood, walking past Coach who gave her a not-subtle-in-the-least thumbs up, heading straight back to the empty row where Nate sat listening to his ear buds. She sat next to him, but he had his eyes closed. She looked closer. Asleep? He'd fallen asleep with his chin on his chest and one earbud dangling from his lobe.

She gently plucked this from him and started to put it into her ear when Nate caught her hand. He looked at her for a long moment and Amanda felt her face color. She dropped the bud. "Sorry," she said, smiling apologetically. "I was just curious."

Nate nodded and pulled out the other one. Amanda had a fleeting thought that he was going to offer both of them to her, but he reached into his pocket and switched off the player and rolled the earbuds up and put them away.

"Look," Amanda said, more unsure now than she'd ever been. "I'm sorry I woke you, I'm sorry I was snooping, I was just wondering what you were listening to, that's all."

"From all the way up there?" Nate asked, indicating the seat she'd just left.

"No," Amanda sighed and shook her head. "No, I was moving back here anyway..."

"Why?" He looked at her frankly.

"I... because I wanted... I thought..."

Nate continued to stare at her. His expression unreadable.

"I just thought that we should... talk."

Nate's face might have been carved from marble. She saw no judgment, no anger, nothing at all. It was like staring at someone who was waiting for you to speak your peace out of politeness, rather than interest.

She sighed and picked at an imaginary piece of lint. "I just wanted to ask you about your... retirement."

Billy had the two seats in front of them. He spun around quickly and looked at Nate quizzically. "You're not serious, right?? You got a lot of good years left, man."

"What's going on?" said a deep voice from behind them in the last row. A guy she hadn't even known was lying down back there shot straight up, draping himself over the back of Nate's seat.

"Nate's gonna retire," Billy practically shouted the news. Apparently Billy, as she was learning, had a tendency to be a little... overenthusiastic about, well, absolutely everything.

"I didn't say that," Nate stopped him, but it was too late. Within moments Amanda was surrounded by giant broad-backed men who clustered around Nate. She couldn't see anything but an ocean of dress shirts and the strong smell of men's cologne filling her nostrils.

Coach Johnson came pushing through down the aisle, sending men scattering into rows that had previously been empty. He was no small man himself, but the tension ratcheted up a considerable amount. "What's this I'm hearing, Nate?" he asked, giving every man there a glare that sent most of them back to their seats.

"Nate says he's gonna retire," Billy added helpfully, seeming content to stay right where he was.

Nate shot Amanda a look. A real nasty one, then sank back into his seat with a low moan.

"No!" Amanda had to shout to be heard. Several heads turned in her direction. No, make that every... by now even the attendants were pausing in their endless circling with platters of food. "That's not what he said, it's what I said."

"Why would you retire?" Billy asked, his face screwed up in confusion.

"Not me, I just mean I said it, I'm not retiring. I was asking Nate about retirement, not me. But I'm the one who said it."

Nick scratched his head. "Why would you try to get Nate to retire?"

Amanda floundered for a moment, but a few mumbled "Yoko Ono" comments still reached her ears from several rows away. "I didn't ..."

"Nate, I would appreciate it if you would come to me first about things like this," Coach Johnson said. "If you're upset about being benched, this is not the solution."

"I already told you!" Amanda blurted out before she clamped her hands over her mouth.

Nate was seething. "It was a *private* conversation, just a little 'what if' thing I was contemplating about *someday*!" he shouted to the throng. "It was said in confidence and was only a discussion. I'm not retiring and, Coach, when I do, I promise you'll be the first to know."

Coach Johnson stared at him a moment and transferred his basilisk gaze to Amanda, who was trying to sink into her chair. He nodded once and spoke to the gathered men. "Subject closed. You heard him!"

"I didn't" a voice from all the way up in the front of the plane said in the pause.

"It's a private conversation, BEST LEFT PRIVATE!" Coach shouted while staring at Amanda.

She nodded miserably.

"Let's all sit down before we overload this side of the plane and end up turning left," Coach muttered and went back to his seat.

"It'll do that?" someone asked as the men returned to their seats. "If we all stand in the back, will we go up?"

Amanda looked over at Nate; he had the earbuds back in his ears and was staring straight ahead.

Amanda slunk back to her original seat.

Someone please just crash the plane now...

Chapter 12

The problem with embarrassing yourself in front of the man you're hired to babysit is that you can't just go home and eat ice cream on the couch and watch *Casablanca*.

Amanda let the thought run through her mind as she watched the streets slip past from the taxi window. Nate had put the damn earbuds back in and STILL hadn't looked in her direction.

At least he hadn't made her take her own cab.

In the end. After a looong silence.

In fact, it was highly likely that he would have left her standing there if she hadn't just scrambled into the cab after him when it seemed he wasn't going to answer about whether they were sharing.

A girl had to be bold sometimes.

But it was still going on, that long protracted silence of his. Any longer and he'd have the record for longest silence by an animated creature.

Hell with it, I'm streaming Casablanca.

"Alright, I'm sorry," she said as they wound through residential neighborhoods. "Again. I'm sorry again, or still sorry. Whatever. I'm SORRY, ok?"

He turned his gaze on her and nodded once. "Fine." He turned back so he was facing the driver's head and remained in that position through Denver, as though the man's hat was the most interesting thing he'd seen in a long time. He kept it up until they arrived at his... no, their (but his) front door.

She bolted from the cab the second it stopped. She snatched her bag from the trunk and walked off, pulling it behind her. It caught on the cobblestones and twisted in her hand.

"Hey!" Nate called. Amanda turned, ready to forgive him, ready to start over and forget the entire trip to L.A. had ever taken place. She dropped her bag and spun on one heel.

"You need to pay your half of the cab ride!" Nate called out and threw his own bag, infinitely bigger and heavier than hers, over his shoulder and walked into the house.

"Multi-million-dollar player and he splits a cab ride," she mumbled as she fished into her wallet for a twenty and shoved it ruefully at the cabbie.

"I'll get you change..." he said helpfully, but didn't make any move to do so.

"Forget it!" she yelled to the house. "Forget it! I'm made of money, obviously! I'm living in a mansion, what the hell?"

She stormed off to where her bags were lying on the path to the guesthouse. She picked them up and stomped off. Three steps later, she realized her 'share' of the cab ride was about eight dollars. And she'd bloody left her car in the short-term parking.

Seventeen carefully counted steps later, she discovered she didn't have ice cream and *Casablanca* wasn't available for streaming.

At least there was a beer in the fridge. She looked it for a long time and closed the door quietly on it, in case it exploded.

On the other hand, it was almost 4:30. What else was there to do?

The strangest part of going to bed at 4:30 in the afternoon is actually falling asleep. She flung herself on the bed, a small ball of misery and pity, and suddenly she was woken by headlights glaring through the window.

It had somehow gotten dark and she'd fallen asleep without closing the curtains to the bedroom which faced the driveway. When a car came to the house in the evening, the headlights swept the windows just before they disappeared behind a corner of the building.

It was 8:20, when a car did just that with precision enough to blind her completely when she opened her eyes. Amanda crawled out of bed and staggered to the window to close the drapes. That's when she woke up enough to realize that the car hadn't parked in front of the door, but had taken the circular driveway and parked where it wouldn't be in the way. This suggested someone who planned to stay a while. Someone who knew the layout of the mansion.

She paused, one hand still on the pull for the drapes.

The driver's door opened and Amanda saw a leg. At one end of the leg was a foot encased in a shoe she would kill for, but was probably beyond the ability of most non-professional gymnasts and tightrope walkers to wear. The toes of that foot were scrunched at a 45-degree angle, and the only other contact with the ground was a single pinprick of a heel that rose a good foot to the bottom of the heel in it. Just to keep such an improbable contortion of a foot from coming unwound at the first step, the entire area was wrapped from toe to ankle in a cross-weave leather thong. Think: if gladiators were sluts.

It was impractical, impossible, and likely over-priced—and Amanda wanted a pair.

The other end of the leg went up for a good four and a half feet to the bottom of a black dress that hung just below where that particular leg joined the other. Think: if sluts were sluts.

The woman attached to so much leg and pricey shoes was stepping out of an equally expensive car, and had a spine like flagpole. By the time Amanda's gaze got to the woman's face, she was half ready for the jolt of recognition that shot through her.

She'd seen this woman before. Her name escaped Amanda's memory. It hadn't been important enough at the time, but the face, hell the *legs,* had been draped across several of Jennifer's magazines for expensive clothes she would never have. This was a professional model, one who used to date *a professional football player*.

"Nate's ex is a professional model?" Amanda cried out loud to the woman who walked into the house like she owned it, though thankfully never heard this particularly inane bit of dialogue. "Of freakin' course." She shook her head and seethed at Fate. "Are you freakin' kidding me?"

How the hell could she compete with a woman who was paid millions to look like someone's wet dream? She stared down at herself. She wore the same clothes she'd worn on the plane home. Wrinkled, askew, sweaty. There was even a little mark on the left breast where she'd dribbled champagne, just to complete the classy trailer park look.

She sat heavily on the bed, head in her hands. She nearly jumped out of her skin when her cell phone rang.

She answered warily, not recognizing the number on her caller ID. "Hello?"

"Hey, uh... Amanda. This is Billy, Billy Bartock, I'm uh..."

"Hey, Billy," Amanda said, "thanks for helping me out yesterday. I thought that security guard was going to throw me out."

"Oh! Right!" Billy laughed.

Amanda could feel the tension, but had no clue why. Was he still upset about the retirement thing? "I think Nate's probably busy right now, Billy..." *Or maybe he's about to get busy?* Amanda stomped on that stray thought.

"No, I, uh... I called to talk to ... I wanted to call you."

Amanda stared at the phone like she expected it to explain things to her. Maybe act as translator if it happened to speak football jock. "Me?"

"Yeah," Billy said then paused. "I know it's late but I thought you might like to get some dinner um...tonight? Or sometime if tonight doesn't work."

"Uh, Billy, I would love to, but..." *But what? But I'm supposed to be Nate's girlfriend and I have to carry on this deception while he has sex with a super-model? Well, yes, that's my excuse.* Nate had been a true bastard since... well since... when hadn't he been?

She needed some time to be Amanda Jones. No job could expect you to change your life and be on call 24/7/365. Billy seemed nice in a rather mountainous kind of way.

She took a deep breath. "That sounds great, Billy."

"Really?!" It was cute how he sounded surprised. "How about I meet you in an hour? There's a great Chinese place I know near the mall."

Amanda had just enough time to shower and dress. Billy was a good guy.

What could go wrong? After all, it wasn't like hanging out with the fabulous, infamous T.N.T.

Chapter 13

Even with showering and calling a cab, Amanda arrived before Billy did. He didn't see her right away, but Billy in a Chinese restaurant was like finding an Easter Island statue in a preschool. He kinda stuck out.

Built like a Humvee on legs, his shoulders were too wide to fit through the door, so he had to cheat and enter sideways while ducking. It was fascinating to watch, really. Amanda couldn't figure out how that much chest could sit atop a thin waist, but something in the way he moved suggested that when training was over, Billy was going to grow a gut. When that happened, he'd probably be even scarier.

He spotted her at the table and grinned like a little boy and wiggled his fingers at her the way a child did when told to greet his grandmother. It was cute and little surreal. He wound his way past the tables, surprisingly graceful, and managed not to trod on anyone. When he sat in the chair opposite her, he ignored the groan of protest from the wood and Amanda, after a moment's panic, accepted that the chair wasn't going to implode after all. At least, not all at once.

"Hey, sorry I'm late," Billy said and ducked his head. Amanda wasn't sure, given how dark his skin was, but thought Billy was blushing. He was nervous. This muscle-bound giant was shy around her.

It was kind of adorable.

She smiled, trying to put him at ease. "I had to make a stop on the way here. So I just got here. You're looking really good today."

Billy grinned, delighted. "Thank you!" He glanced down at his button-down shirt, tucked casually into a pair of jeans. "It's kinda hard finding clothes for someone my size; most of what I have I had to get tailor-made. If I had a regular job, I couldn't afford any clothing at all."

Amanda smiled, not sure how to respond to that, and pretended to study the menu. Billy *did* study the menu and spent a great deal of time before choosing two of the meals out of the four front-runners. He folded the menu and smiled beatifically at her.

"So," he said, leaning forward on the table, tilting it dangerously in his direction. "How's Nate?"

Talking about one's pretend boyfriend was not what Amanda was expecting on a first date, but sure... why not? "Nate is... good. I think. I'm not sure, as he's not actually talking to me at the moment. After what happened on the plane." She sighed. "I don't do well on planes, I think."

"Nonsense," Billy said with a gentle smile. "You were fine. In fact, I really liked the underwear."

She choked on the water she was sipping. "Uh...thank you."

"No, it was cute. Not everyone can pull off a thong and a fall like that." Amanda felt her face heat up. It didn't help when Billy added. "I certainly can't."

The visual was too much for her. Amanda hid behind the menu before she did something totally asinine like laugh and hurt his feelings. But the image stayed with her.

What the hell? These football players were going to be the death of her.

When the waiter came, Billy waffled again and decided on all four entrées. Amanda simply stared at him. "Where are you going to put that much food?"

Billy shook his head. "Listen, we're in training all day every day. If the nutritionist knew what I was doing here tonight, she'd get on her broom and write 'Surrender Dorothy' over my house.

The problem is, we burn a lot of calories and we need to take in a lot, too. I work out six hours a day when we don't have a game. That's a lot of fuel."

"Well, it really shows," Amanda said, trying to take back a little of the unintended criticism. "You look great."

"Thanks." Billy pulled a pair of chopsticks out of the container in the center of the table and snapped them apart idly. They looked like toothpicks in his hands. He tapped them on the table, using them as impromptu drumsticks for a short solo that involved a bottle of soy sauce, the napkin dispenser, and his silverware.

Amanda laughed and applauded his efforts, and he ducked his head, doing that embarrassed thing again.

"What do you mean, he's not talking to you?" he asked, dropping the chopsticks on the table.

Amanda sighed. She was pretty sure she'd been able to steer the conversation away from that, even if she did risk insulting him about his appetite. "I don't know. I mean... I shouldn't have said anything to him about the retirement thing on the plane. That was stupid of me. I just... I wasn't thinking, you know? And I probably shouldn't have let on to the rest of the team that I was hired to pretend to be his girlfriend either."

"It was a surprise," Billy said, his tone serious.

"I know, I know. I just. I feel like I've done everything wrong. I open my mouth and out comes something else I shouldn't say, or I try to fit in and look like a cheap hooker."

"You've had a busy week." Billy nodded, not unkindly.

"You don't know the half of it." She groaned. "I never thought that inviting my cousin to a game would put me in trouble either!"

"Yeah, Nate was kinda put out by that," Billy agreed. "That's why he left the field."

If it was possible, Amanda's jaw hit the floor. "*That's* why he left? It can't be." The look on Billy's face confirmed. She buried her face in her hands. "That can't be why he's leaving the team."

"So he *is* quitting, then? It's not just something he's talking about?"

Amanda peered out from the circle of her arms. "See? I did it again!" She shook her head slowly. "I don't think he wants to retire, Billy, I just think he found a way out of a bad deal and he's desperate enough to take it. He doesn't want me, Billy; he doesn't want this charade, either."

"Have you asked him what he does want?"

Amanda was saved from answering by the arrival of their food. While she scrambled to move her water glass and utensils to make room on the table, she thought frantically. She'd presumed that Coach had talked to Nate. No, if she was to be honest, she hadn't given it any thought at all.

"I suppose not," she admitted when the waiter had found room for all four plates. Billy tore into the kung pao chicken like it was going to be taken away if he didn't beat the clock. Amanda picked at her food as best she could in the limited area allotted to her plate. "I don't suppose it occurred to me to talk to him."

"Maybe you should?" Billy asked as he finish the kung pao and started on the chow Mein crispy noodles.

"I think it's too late," she said sadly, pushing at her broccoli beef with a chopstick.

"Never too late," Billy said around a healthy mouthful.

"Yeah, I think it is. When I left my apartment, a pair of legs attached to a blonde showed up. I think I remember her..."

"Alanna's back?" Billy almost didn't get his mouth around the name and the orange chicken at the same time.

That was it, Alanna Roysvic. Something like that. Supermodel, known for her 'pensive' look that, to Amanda's mind, was more a disapproving constipation than anything even remotely thoughtful. She was in every magazine but *Popular*

Science and had been featured in the latest *Victoria's Secret* catalog. Not that she shopped from there or anything.

"I'm such as idiot," Amanda said and gave up on the chopsticks completely as a broccoli floret dropped to her plate for the fourth time. "There's a high-class underwear model in his... house." She fumbled for the fork, then stared in disbelief as she dropped that selfsame bit of broccoli off the end of her fork. This time it hit the edge of the table and kept on going until it was halfway across the table.

"Yeah, she probably came because of the paper," Billy said, halfway through his third entrée. He showed signs of slowing down, though. A bit. Or that he was reaching for the food she'd dropped.

"What paper?" she asked, giving up on the idea of eating altogether since it seemed utensils were entirely beyond her tonight.

Billy held up a finger and stood. He slipped through the restaurant and out the front door. Only then did Amanda realize that the rest of the diners were watching them and two of the staff in the back of the place had $20 bills out, wagering on whether Billy could finish everything he ordered.

He returned a moment later with a copy of the Denver Post. "There's a machine outside," he said by way of explanation. He tossed everything but the sports section and there, on the front page of that portion of the paper was...her. In L.A. Jumping up with her arms in the air and her tits all the way up to her chin and off to the right.

Bouncing Broncos Girl linked to two players and mystery date.

Amanda shoved the plate away from her completely. "Bouncing Broncos Girl?" Her voice rose on each word until it was halfway to the stratosphere. "I just sent women back to the suffragette movement." She buried her head in her hands for the second time that night.

"Listen," Billy said. "Don't take it so hard. Remember, your love affair with Nate isn't real. Alanna isn't good for him, never was, but she'll keep him out of the papers."

"What do you mean 'not good for him'?" Amanda asked, lifting her head.

"She uses people. Not for money, she's got plenty of that, but she needs someone on her arm who will boost her career and make her look good. Having a famous football player on your arm looks good in the papers."

"On her arm or under her impractical heels?"

Billy shrugged and speared an egg roll with his chopstick. "Whatever. Nate was always a worse screw-up with her, but she never allowed it to get known. She kept him from the papers and from getting noticed unless he was with her. Owners didn't much like it either. They were losing publicity, losing tickets. They broke them up."

Amanda blinked. "How did *they* break them up?"

"Offered her a fat contract in another country. She left to go look good on a beach somewhere and met a local who is as gorgeous as she is." Billy thought a moment and added, "and slightly more feminine."

"But not famous," Amanda added.

"No, not famous."

Billy ate while Amanda thought. So... Alanna was back to re-hook Nate.

"Billy," Amanda asked, "if you're so concerned about Nate, why did you ask me out?"

Billy set his chopsticks down. Amanda thought they had to be pretty warm from all that friction by now. He looked around; the two waiters had almost finished their bet, but they were out of earshot. The rest of the place had gotten over the shock of having a famous football player in the same restaurant with them.

"I was just thinking," Billy said, leaning forward in what she supposed he might have thought was a subtle move, had it not sent half the plates skidding toward his edge of the table.

Amanda lunged at the same moment Billy did, clunking heads as they saved what was left of dinner in a wild clatter of dishes that brought the staff running. Billy quit leaning on the table and raised his hands, showing that everything was all right.

Amanda just about died of embarrassment for the...how many times had it been today?

Billy waited until everyone was out of earshot before speaking again.

"Now that I know Alanna is in town, she'll keep him out of the tabloids, or he'll quit. Then what plans do you have?"

"What do you mean?"

"Well, the apartment is in Nate's house, you'll have to move, you'll have no job... What are your plans?"

"I guess... I really hadn't thought about further plans, really..." *Oh good one, girl. Here's something you should have considered...*

"I would like to hire you," Billy said grandly.

"To do what?"

"Be my girlfriend, obviously."

Amanda threw her napkin down on the table. "I am NOT a prostitute!" she snapped, and shot to her feet.

"No, no, no no..." Billy stood, too, and towered over her, waving his hands. "I didn't mean that, I really didn't mean that at all. Amanda, it's me! Billy! You know me, sorta. Would I do something like that to you?"

Amanda stared at him with something between a venomous hate-filled glare, and an old-fashioned girl pout. She sat. And stared.

Billy looked around to be sure he couldn't be heard. "I need..." he whispered. He switched to the chair beside her. One of the waiters reached for the other $20 and they started an argument over Billy being done or taking a break. "I need..." Billy said so softly she almost didn't hear him. His nose nearly touched hers. "... a beard." He sighed as though a great relief had passed through his giant frame.

"A what?" she asked flatly. It was the most incongruous thing she'd ever heard. He might have said 'penguin' for all the sense it made.

"A beard." He pronounced it bee-ard, drawing out the syllables as though it has some specific meaning.

"Stop shaav-ing then," she said just as quietly.

Billy shook his head.

Amanda shrugged and watched him.

He reached into his pocket and pulled out his phone. He pressed a few buttons and showed her the screen.

Beard

Beard is a **slang** term describing a person who is used, knowingly or unknowingly, as a date, romantic partner (boyfriend or girlfriend), or spouse to conceal one's sexual orientation.

"Oh." Realization came on her in a rush. "Ohhh! You're g... you... I mean ... oh..."

"Look," Billy said quietly, "you don't have a great success rate with secrets, but this one is very important. I shower with a dozen guys. I'm in a very good-old-boy profession. Please, if you've ever kept a secret in your life let it be this one?"

"This I can. This is no one's business but your own." Hadn't she thought that briefly about Nate? She smiled at Billy. "All the good ones are, you know?" Amanda couldn't have sounded more idiotic if she'd tried.

Billy tossed his napkin onto the table. One of the waiters snatched the bill from his companion, much to the muttering of the latter.

"Can we get some to-go containers, please?" Billy called.

The losing waiter tried to snatch the bill back. They fell into the kitchen, arguing.

Amanda needed a moment. To recap the situation. The day. Or whatever the hell she needed. She was a nose in a book kind of girl. There was way too much action for this girl in one day. *The man you slept with, and apparently have feelings for, is hooked up with a dominatrix supermodel. The closest thing you have to a friend right now is a 350-pound African-American version of the Hulk crossed with a drag queen. And you are now known as the* Bouncing Broncos Girl *because your titties tried to fly on camera.* What now?

In answer to her internal lament, her phone vibrated in her purse. It was a text message. Warily she extracted the phone, halfway convinced it was about to explode. It'd been that kind of day.

You let my car get towed? Seriously? I know I said you could keep it, but seriously? George.

Who knew? For once she'd called it.

"CHECK PLEASE!" she yelled in the general direction of the kitchen, then turned to Billy. "Do you know where I can rent *Casablanca?*"

"I have three copies. You can have one."

Suddenly the 'Surrender Dorothy' comment made sense.

Chapter 14

Bogart had just claimed that, "If she can stand it, I can. Play it!" when the phone rang. Amanda paused just before Sam struck up the song. She wanted to hear "As Time Goes By" from the beginning.

It was the land line, the one that went through Nate's house, the one that never rang unless it was him or Coach Johnson. It was hardly likely either would be calling at 11PM with good news.

"I would like to talk to you. Now," Nate said as soon as she picked up. "Please."

She waited, listening to him breathe. "Okay," she said finally and hung up the phone. She'd kept the clothes on from her dinner with Billy, with the concession of taking off her shoes (sensible and flat, of course). She slipped them back on and thanked Ben and Jerry for their help, setting the remains back in the freezer.

She took a deep breath, trying to still the butterflies in her belly, and walked out of the guest house, shoulders back and head straight. She spent the short walk certain the sprinklers would fire off at any moment. Or there would be a sinkhole that opened under her feet. Actually, she was praying for the sinkhole.

Sadly, the short journey was uneventful and she didn't need to be spirited away in an ambulance and thus tragically be unable to face him. *Damn, I should write romance novels.* She took a deep breath and rang the bell.

Nate opened the door a minute later and it occurred to her that she'd not been in the main house yet. He invited her into a cavern of white paint and marble, arching staircases that swooped like angel wings to an upper floor. Awards stood poised on every wall and flat surface.

He led her into a sitting room of sorts and plopped down on a couch that must have cost as much as her parents' house in The Springs. "Please," he indicated a chair next to the couch, "have a seat."

It was like being called into the principal's office. Or worse, a lawyer who was all smiles and happiness because he'd found a way to hurt you badly. She was hired to tame the wild child, but she'd lost that upper hand somewhere.

Nate handed her a folded newspaper. The sports section.

She cringed. "I've seen it."

"Have you read it?"

"No," Amanda admitted, studying her nails that she'd somehow bitten down to a point no manicure could save. "Billy just showed it to me."

"Billy?" Nate sat up. "When did you see Billy?"

Her head shot up. "About an hour ago. We had dinner."

"Great, that can be in tomorrow's paper then." He slumped back on the couch, throwing a pillow across the room for good measure.

"Hey, just because I was hired to keep you out of the papers, which, I may point out to you, I have done..."

Nate stood and waved the paper at her.

"That's me, not you!" she yelled, yanking the paper from his grip and using it to swat him on the shoulder. Hard.

"READ IT!" Nate yelled back.

Amanda stood up and faced him, the newspaper crumpled in her hand. "You do NOT get to dictate my actions! I'll live my life as I please, thank you very much!"

"Not when you're SUPPOSED to be MY girl!"

"Tell that to your supermodel fuck figure! I mean, stick figure!"

"I DID!" Nate yelled. "THAT'S WHY SHE LEFT!"

"WELL FINE!" Amanda screamed back.

Then suddenly there seemed to be a missing piece of awareness, a glitch in her timeline.

One minute she was screaming at Nate, then the next she had both legs wrapped around his waist and her hands in his thick sandy hair and was covering him with kisses while he held her effortlessly, his hands running up and down her spine, under the blouse and to the bra clasp.

She felt the clasp pop and his hand ran along her skin, heating and touching. Caressing her body. She moaned into his mouth and viciously pulled at his shirt. She thought she might have gotten hit by a button, but she wasn't sure and didn't care anyway.

His naked, broad chest, and wide shoulders felt as wonderful as she remembered from the beach. She climbed down off him long enough to let him rip her shirt and bra off over her head. Without giving herself much time to think about it, she pushed him back on the couch, falling with him. Her mouth trailed hard, biting, passionate kisses from his nape to his navel before a daring little thought snuck in that left her attacking his belt and tearing open his pants.

She ripped them down, he rose to assist, but her fingers betrayed her need. She left long scratches down his thighs and stared a long moment at the beautiful flesh rising right before her very eyes. Oral sex had been neither desired nor avoided with her; it had never mattered one way or another in the past. She'd been on the giving end only once and the whole thing had left her feeling rather 'meh' about it. But with Nate, she had to have him.

She dove right in, mouth eagerly taking, and was surprised at how aroused it left her to feel the weight of him on her tongue. She experimented a little, tasting, sucking, even scraping her teeth along the length of him and discovered that she loved the feel of him. The taste of him left her hungry for more. The experience was like nothing she'd ever experienced before.

He lay back and ran his fingers through her hair and worked her head over his shaft, still hardening, still thickening as she sucked and licked. Her head bobbed up and down over him as his hands, his strong, warm, huge hands stroked her back and head and shoulders and neck, and even reached around and caressed and stroked her nipples. She moaned, matching his own groan as he swelled even larger. Her jaw began to ache from the sheer width of the man.

Then just when she felt a pulse at the base of the shaft, when she thought he would explode in her mouth, leaving her with the dilemma of pulling away or swallowing—something she had never done before—he pulled her head away and shoved her backwards so that she sprawled on the floor next to the couch, her legs splayed and open to him. She lay there, half dazed, breathing heavily, meeting his eyes with a question, wondering how it was that he was able to stop at this point. Then the question was answered as he dragged her skirt down over her hips, then with one hand grabbed her panties and tore them from her body, shredding them in his grasp. She gasped as her wet pussy was exposed to the chill air.

He moved her over him so she was straddling his mouth, facing away from him, so that his tongue—his oh-so-sweet tongue—could fire into her heat, splitting her open and driving hard and fast into her slit over and over and over. She fell and her head landed on his thigh. His thick cock was there, and she had just sucked it into her mouth when she came.

She spasmed, her thighs pressed against his face. She didn't know if he could breathe, but she couldn't stop, couldn't move as she came and came. She buried her screams around his beautiful cock, opening her mouth and throat with the climax and using him to muffle her cries. She parted her thighs and rose to let him breathe, only to find her own breath blocked by his huge, throbbing shaft. With a shocked laugh, she lifted her head to get some air and saw his toes a million miles away. Not satisfied with the view, she spun as soon as her legs would respond.

Damn, he was amazing.

She stared at him lying there on the floor, naked, erect...an Adonis. He was Michelangelo's David, hard and eager. She mounted him, sitting tall upon him, sliding his thickness into her heat so that she could ride him. With her hands on his chest, pressing him down, using him to balance, she lifted and fell, then lifted and fell over and over. Her breasts ached from the bouncing, her thighs burned from the exercise she was forcing on them, but he felt so good....so fucking good.

The burn, the aches, all faded or became a part of the mounting climax, the heat, the friction, the stretching of her around him...the chiseled look of him made her arch against the pleasure. Yet another climax started deep in her core.

He called out, wordless, blinded by his own climax. His hands reached up and grabbed her breasts, squeezing, mauling. His shaft throbbed in her, pulsing, and she came. She shuddered around his release, her aching thighs shaking from exertion as her torso bucked and strained under the climax that blinded her to all but a single receding pinprick of light that smelled and tasted and looked like Nate.

She collapsed on top of him, chest heaving as she tried to catch her breath, her legs now intertwined with his, her arm holding her pressed to him. He was heaving with the exertion, too.

When she looked at him, he seemed as dazed and glassy-eyed as she felt.

He met her gaze, looking at her there on top of him. Finally, he lifted one hand and took her wrist in his grasp. His fingers swallowed her tiny wrist. He could have caused her pain, could have crushed her wrist, but his touch was delicate. And though he was holding her firmly, he wasn't holding her at all tightly. If she pulled away now, he'd release her in an instant. Somehow, she knew this.

"Don't run away," he said, his voice low, husky. "Not this time."

Amanda blinked back tears, suddenly overwhelmed. How did one respond to so much naked emotion? Finally, she bit her lower lip and nodded. "Can we move to a bed?" she asked, her voice barely more than a whisper.

He stood and helped her to her feet. Her knees seemed still somewhat confused on which way they were supposed to bend. She slipped out of the remnants of what used to be her underwear then reached for his hand.

Why did it have to be so surprising when he took it? She ducked her head, letting her hair fall in a cascade down to cover her burning cheeks.

Now I'm shy?

"You know what the best part of being with a professional athlete is?" he asked, lifting one hand to brush back the errant strands, tucking them gently behind her ear.

She looked up at him. Shook her head in mute response when she couldn't get her voice to work.

He grinned. This was the Nate Thomas the world knew. That wicked boy/man who could melt your kneecaps with a single smile. He bent close, and whispered the answer in her ear, "Recovery time."

Almost afraid to look, she let her eyes drop to his waist. Then lower.

"Oh, fuck," she whispered, her mouth suddenly dry. "You do know that I'm not a professional athlete, right?"

Nate scooped her up in his arms and carried her up the soaring staircase and into his bedroom.

Chapter 15

When she woke, Amanda knew that this time she wasn't going to be able to slip away like she'd done on the beach. Nate was thoroughly on top of her, legs entwined with hers; his heavy, thick arms were wrapped around her. His head lay on the pillow above hers so her head was nestled just under his jaw.

They'd actually slept that way. It was like she'd tried to catch a falling giant, he covered her so completely. For a moment, she imagined what it would have been like to wake with Billy like this and she shuddered. It would take days before a rescue party would find her under that bulk. No, Nate was just right, big enough to feel... well, to feel completely wrapped up in someone, but not so big as to feel like she would just disappear without a trace.

I still want to hide.

She breathed deeply, a part of her reveling in the moment. The other part was screaming at her that it would be better to slink away. To finish her Ben and Jerry's and to hear "As Time Goes By" once more. Why would she want to stay for the inevitable awkward morning-after moment, when Nate realized he'd thrown away a supermodel for a super nerd? He was going to do his best to hide his disappointment, she was sure. But it would be there when morning light sobered him up, the way it had with other men when they realized what they'd done, or promised, in the throes of passion.

She didn't want to see that again. She especially didn't want to see it in his eyes. Especially not with him. Maybe she could bolt if she was careful. Quiet. She could pack her things and just go...

well, somewhere. *I could go to the airport and fly away, far away, go see my parents and hide in their basement.* She made a mental note to pick up the *Casablanca* DVD on the way out.

But more than that she wanted... well, she wanted to pee. Very, very badly.

Nate was fast asleep.

The thought crossed her mind of what he looked like when he slept. From here all she could see was shoulder and muscle. She lay there, determined to ignore the ever-pressing need of her bladder. The bathroom was basically at the foot of the bed, a few scant feet away.

Her resolve lasted almost two minutes.

She lifted his arm, carefully, so slowly, and placed it on his hip. Damn, he was gorgeous. She raised up and lifted his leg off hers and slid out from under him, all while holding her breath. She rose as quietly as she could and turned to stare down at him. He was fun to look at, and asleep he looked, if anything, more intense.

She padded to the bathroom and closed the door, stealing a glance at herself in the mirror, seeing the strange woman with tousled hair and soft eyes. No, her bladder wasn't giving her time for self-recrimination, she had too much pressure built up. When she was done, on the other hand, her bladder didn't care and allowed her all the time in the world to wallow in her guilt.

Amanda wasn't even sure who exactly was looking out at her from the mirror when she looked again. There was something of a wild creature in the tangles that framed her face. Her lips were parted slightly, still swollen from a night of passionate kisses. When she turned, she caught a glimpse of a mark on her neck that had her freeze in absolute shock.

A hickey? He'd given her a hickey?

Somehow that made it all worse.

This oddly ravenous creature who got hickeys, who indulged in wild crazy sex, had to go. Before she did something insane like go back in the other room and start nibbling bits until he woke up just to see if he was up for a round of do-overs. Because, you know, they might not have done it right last night.

No. That wouldn't do. The part of her brain that had wanted to flee was winning quickly.

She splashed water on her face and tried to comb out her hair with the small plastic comb she found in a drawer, but the bedhead from the night before wasn't about to be tamed that easily. She tried to comb it with wet fingers, thinking that might work better, and all she got was the beginnings of a headache.

With a sigh and no small amount of trepidation, she turned off the lights and tiptoed back into the bedroom only to stand in confusion when she realized there was no sign of her clothing anywhere. She was kneeling next to the bed, trying to see if anything had perhaps been kicked under there, when she remembered that everything was probably still in the living room.

"You promised you wouldn't run away this time."

He didn't even open his eyes. For all the look of him, he could have been talking in his sleep. She stood there wondering what the odds were that he just so happened to have a dream with those same words at the exact moment that she...

Amanda sighed. Yeah.

She got up and eased back into the bed, lying down beside him in more or less the same position she had been in before. His arm and leg encircled her again and his chin nestled in her hair. Her heart was pounding a million miles an hour. "I was trying to find a blanket," she whispered after a moment. "It's cold."

He released her again. "If you can find it, go ahead."

She did find one, over on the other end of the room formed into a little nest from the night before. She blushed as she remembered creating that space. She pulled it up over the bed and reluctantly covered his form before lying down again, this time facing away from him.

He pulled her to him and wrapped her up again in his limbs.

Amanda stiffened a moment and then realized she was being held by one of the most beautiful men she'd ever seen. Why fight it? He wanted her there and, honestly, she wanted to be there. More than running away, more even than *Casablanca*. She nestled into him and let herself sleep better than she had in months. Morning could take care of itself. Besides, she'd promised, hadn't she?

She was sure she wouldn't sleep so much as a minute, but then she was waking and alone in the giant bed. Daylight seeped around the cracks of the heavy curtains and she sat up, trying to figure out whether he'd merely gone to the bathroom, or had defected to Russia, when the door opened and the twin smells of coffee and toast proceeded him into the room. He hadn't bothered getting dressed.

He looked kind of cute, naked and holding a serving tray, and she couldn't help but giggle. She sat up and fought the urge to cover herself with the blankets. It was one thing to strip in the heat of the moment, but to sit exposed in the unforgiving light of day was unnerving. Still, he was setting the tone, so she gamely complied.

The toast was simple, butter and some jam, but it was a heavy wheat and had nuts and seeds.

"This is really good," she said around a mouthful.

"It's on the diet list," he said, biting into his own.

She blinked then sat back to take a good look at him. A very good look. There wasn't an ounce of fat on him. "You're on a diet?"

"The whole team is. Not losing weight, but we have a list of things we're supposed to eat and how often and how much."

"Right," she said, blushing because it was the sort of thing she felt she should have known. "Because you burn so many calories."

"Yeah," he smiled and nudged her with his shoulder, "and you and I burned off a few last night, so eat up."

If anything, Amanda blushed even deeper, though she hadn't thought that was possible until now. She ducked her head and bit into the bread like she was told. "Can I ask what happened with Allanna?" she asked after she'd chewed and swallowed. Maybe it wasn't the best morning-after conversation, but she wasn't going to sit easy until she had a clearer understanding of things. Better to get all the nasty things out of the way now, while she could still bolt with some semblance of dignity.

"You recognized her?"

Amana snorted. "Not that hard to miss, she's on every checkout register in the supermarkets."

"Yeah. She saw the paper and wanted to get back together. Seems that now that I have some publicity again, she wanted to use that to boost her image. It keeps her in demand if she's always in the news, you know."

"So, what happened?"

"I told her I already had a girlfriend and that she was living with me. She told me to trot you out to meet her, I told her to go to hell. We compromised: she left, and I didn't take a bat to her car. It worked out best for us both."

Amanda blinked. "You didn't have to. I mean if you're retiring anyway, what difference does it make to keep up the façade?"

Nate pulled the covers off her lap, exposing her.

"HEY!"

"Just checking," he said, and pulled them back over her legs.

"For what?"

"Well, I think I can absolutely state that you are, in fact, a girl."

Amanda blushed and bit into her toast before she said something she regretted.

"And, considering the events of last night, I would say that you and I have some sort of relationship, so I don't think I exactly *lied* to her, did I?"

"But she's so pretty." Amanda was getting flustered. "She's a *supermodel*. I'm just..."

"You're just...?"

She carefully set the toast down on the plate. "... Me." The word came out in a whisper. Suddenly there weren't enough blankets in the world to hide under.

Nate leaned over and kissed her nose. "Let's just stay naked today. We have a big house, a stocked refrigerator, and an Olympic-sized pool." He smiled that mischievous grin and turned it into a challenge.

Amanda took a shaky breath. A tiny part of her unfolded, much like a flower coming into bloom. "Well, what the hell," she said finally, shrugging and even laughing a little. "OK. I seem to be naked around you a lot anyway."

Nate smiled and kissed a little stray jam from her cheek. The look he gave her was pure dynamite.

Damned if she wasn't ready to see what blew up next.

Chapter 16

The day after a game was supposed to be used to recover from said game. There were no practices, no exercises to do, no meetings of team members to discuss strategies and plays. In laymen's terms, 'a day off.'

Amanda was just a little uncertain about spending a day without dressing, in the way a turkey might be uncertain about Thanksgiving. She kept seeing that long leg in her memory, and it got longer and leaner with every passing moment.

She stood in front of a mirror on tiptoes, trying to see what effect it would have on her. She liked the way that it looked, she decided. High heels stretched out the leg, firmed up the ass. She tried turning to see how it looked from the front, but decided against it when she fell on the carpet.

She was on her feet quickly, before he stepped back into the room wondering what 'that noise' was. She looked around and tried to not pay attention to the heat rising in her face.

"So..." she shrugged, naked... *Naked!* In front of him. This was getting too...

"Let's take a shower," he suggested, nodding past her to the enclosure that passed for such a thing in his bathroom. She'd never seen so many shower heads in her life. For that matter, she'd never been in a shower that could comfortably take a half dozen people and leave room for soaping...and whatever.

Of course, it being the famous TNT's shower, this led to her wondering whether the shower had been put to just such a use already.

The whole thing was unnerving. Made worse by the fact that he was staring at her and waiting for her response.

"Sure!" As far as chirpy responses better suited to cheerleaders, it wasn't half bad until she caught a glimpse of her face in the mirror. She looked like she was having an aneurism.

There were more controls than her car had. The hot water was a bit too hot, and she tried to slip it down a notch when he wasn't looking. He yelped as the icy water hit him. This led to a good-natured tussle until they found a temperature they could both appreciate with no small amount of laughing. Somehow in there she managed to activate something that made the gentle rainfall from overhead turn into a downpour of hurricane proportions. He retaliated by introducing the heads built into the sides of the shower until she cried mercy, thinking she'd seen less water the last time she'd taken her sedan through the car wash.

Finally, half-drowned, a truce was declared and they got down to the serious business of getting clean.

Nate worked up a lather in his hands, all while eyeing Amanda speculatively. She backed away, suddenly unsure. He caught her anyway, taking her in his arms under the spray as he soaped her back and worked his way down her spine to her ass. He clenched her buttocks in his strong hands while the steam rose around them, and for the life of her she couldn't remember what she'd been running from.

He soaped her ass, her thighs, and went to one knee to wash her shins. His face was at her crotch and he leaned in to take advantage of the position. His tongue weakened her knees as his hands spread the remaining soap on them. She grabbed his head and held him as he slipped his tongue into her and played with her nub.

Kissing upward, he licked her belly and breasts and took a nipple into his mouth as his hands spread the soap where his tongue had just been. He pulled on the nipple, teasing it, nibbling at it with his teeth and tormenting her with his tongue while his fingers washed her slit. He stood and worked the lather into her breasts, his thumbs flattening and flicking her sensitive nipples.

Amanda had no idea how she was staying upright and clung to him, fingernails digging into his shoulders as he took the shower head and washed her front and back and then poured the water over her head. She wasn't ready for that particular attack and came up sputtering, swatting his hands away until she could wipe the water from her eyes. He paid no attention to her protestations and took the shampoo and lathered it into her scalp, briskly rubbing it in, massaging her head.

It was intimate.

Arousing.

She was honestly surprised. Sex between them had been all explosions and mad passion. Now, standing under the warm spray with his hands running over her body, she discovered something else: the low steady throb of passion just beneath the surface. The way her skin was positively humming as he moved his hands over her.

The way she wanted this to go on forever, coupled with the need to touch him in the same way.

The soap ran down the drain, cascading down between her breasts. Slipping between her ass cheeks in silken warmth that left her smoldering. She couldn't take it anymore.

It was her turn.

Amanda looked him up and down with more than a hint of speculation. She'd read something once...though it was way outside of her comfort zone.

Okay, what part of this is IN my comfort zone?

With that thought in mind, she took the soap and created a great deal of lather, but she didn't put it on him. Instead she spread it liberally over her breasts. Then, holding her breath, she stepped into his embrace, rubbing herself over him. Her tight, aching nipples smashed up against his hard, muscular chest. Her hands grabbed his ass as he had with her, but her breasts were moving over him, and all the careful rinsing he'd done with her was forgotten.

She knelt—squatted really—and trapped his cock between her breasts and pressed them together, rubbing the ripe flesh up and down the length of his cock. It was already hard from the touching and the heat they'd generated, and he gasped and grabbed the shower door to steady himself.

Heady with delight at his reaction, her hand soaped his balls and legs and she turned around and ran her ass cheeks over this part of his body, over his hardness and his belly until she was bent over at waist height. It was a dizzying sensation. She rose once only to snatch the shower head, and hosed him off, taking the time to rinse the soap again from her own body, and presented herself again.

There was no hesitation on his part. She could have sworn he cheered, or at the least gave some sound of satisfaction as he slipped into her. She gasped as he filled her and stood a moment, adjusting, before she realized she still held the shower hose in her hand. He moved against her and the hose shifted and moved as she did, sending the spray shooting up between her legs. It hit her clit and her eyes shot open in surprise at the measure of delight. From that point on she held it there, driving needles of hot water over her most sensitive of spots as he pushed into her and filled her again.

This time when he slammed home, she almost dropped the shower head. As it was, the water shot wildly into his face, but he only crashed into her harder for it. With the choice fast becoming that of bracing herself somehow or falling on her face and drowning, she dropped the hose and pressed her palms against the tiled wall as he grasped her hips and pumped into her again.

The nozzle of the forgotten hose sped across the floor of the shower, spraying water in every direction as he slammed in and out in and out. At random, warm water sprayed them or the wall or the door and she cried out and came hard, her sex pulling his, trapping his cock with her throbbing core. He gave a shout and slammed home one last time. She felt him pulse inside of her, his whole body rocking and shaking with the spasms of his own orgasm as he held her against him.

She fumbled for the hose, still curling around the floor of the shower like a wild thing, and rinsed his cock one more time, following up with an impish lick along the length of it before rising and washing the residue off her breasts.

He stood there, one hand on the tiled wall just over her head, eyes closed, breathing hard. For once the athlete had been sated.

Her own hands were shaking as she moved them over the various knobs. Finally, she had the water turned off and faced him, her own chest heaving, her body aching pleasantly and more than clean. She looked at him, somewhat wide-eyed as she tried to process the whole thing and gave up, rising on tiptoe to plant a tender kiss upon his lips.

And immediately regretted it.

After a night of passion, a morning of blatant nudity, and now a shower from a porno, suddenly the kiss—the *kiss* made her shy. He hadn't made a move toward her. There quite honestly had been no reaction at all.

Amanda panicked.

There was nothing to blame this on. No heat of the moment, nothing.

This was a kiss that meant more than sex, more than need. It meant something important and it came from her.

She realized what she'd done and wanted to flee. Her hand went to the door, one footstep back.

Then he smiled.

Amanda blushed and threw the door open, grabbing the first towel she saw. The sudden realization that he had dumped a supermodel for... *her* was too much. None of this was real. It couldn't be real. It couldn't be happening to her.

What if it is?

And for just a moment... she let herself believe it.

After all, logic told her Ben and Jerry weren't selling hallucinogenic ice cream. Maybe she wasn't destined to wake up from this dream with a sugar hangover and the main menu from the *Casablanca* DVD waiting for her to push a button?

She buried her face in the towel, ignoring the fact that he was there, right behind her, and asking her more than once if she was okay. She was shaking.

This whole situation was just funny, hilariously funny. But in a weird, strange, stupid way that no one could possibly understand.

Nate was holding her, his voice starting to sound panicked. He thought she was crying and he was worried, and it was so sweet and nice that she dropped her towel. Her eyes met his, seeing the confusion and a small bit of fear in his eyes before she blurted out, "I suck at babysitting," and dissolved into a bad case of the giggles.

Nate spanked her ass hard.

Amanda doubled over, laughing.

Chapter 17

"I wanted to talk to you about dinner," Nate said, looking serious.

"Okay..." She had no idea why his face was so serious.

"There isn't any."

Amanda's stomach growled. This wasn't exactly the best news of the day. Or the worst. Though they had worked up quite the appetite.

Nate shrugged, hands palms-up in a whatcha-gonna-do position. "Look, I don't cook and the nutritionist usually provides food for the team, but the day after a game is a 'free day', so I don't have anything in the house."

Amanda glanced down at herself. A day sans clothes suddenly felt a little problematic. "I'm not opening the door for the pizza guy naked," she said, crossing her arms in front of her. Then she noticed the effect it had on him as she lifted her breasts like that. Nice as that was and all, she still blushed and dropped her hands to her sides. No, not exactly comfortable with any of it yet.

He stifled a laugh. "Don't worry, I'm not in the mood for pizza." He leaned over and kissed her forehead. "Let's go out and get something."

"Naked?" she teased. "It was your idea to spend the day naked. I just didn't know you meant in public."

"Wouldn't be my first time," Nate said half under his breath.

Amanda chose to ignore that. "Well, I'm going to skip having a first time." She got up and looked around the room. "Though, come to think of it, where did my clothes go when... last night?"

They searched the living room, under the couch, the hallway, the bedroom, but apparently her clothing seemed to have fled the premises. She wound up borrowing a bathrobe amidst his teasing about 'being a party pooper' and padded out the door and across the pathway to the guest house, pausing to stick her tongue out at him from the front door.

She changed into a pair of jeans, a t-shirt, and boots, and took a moment to try to fix her hair. Looking in the mirror was a strange experience. She had no idea who it was who looked back at her. This woman was cute, confident, smiled easily, and Amanda *liked* her. She wanted to *be* that woman and it took her a moment to realize she was.

Her hair hung loose over her shoulders, cascading in a tousled wave. The jeans were just a little tight; she'd never had the confidence to wear them, but it seemed right today somehow. She looked... sexy. Sexual. Sensual.

She took a deep breath, as deep as the jeans would allow, and smiled at that woman.

That's me.

I like me.

When he rang the bell, she ran to meet him, laughing and out of breath as she flung open the door. He smiled and held out his hand to her. Damn, he was adorable. And for today at least... he was hers.

They drove with the top down despite the chill that traced the Denver wind.

She sat leaning against the door, half turned so she could watch him. It was an interesting experience, seeing the double-take of the guy in the truck next to them at the stoplight. The easy way that Nate smiled and waved before taking off.

Playing the celebrity.

Yet she'd seen a different side of him that morning. And in California.

"Nate, can I ask you something?"

He lifted an eyebrow in response.

"Why the act? When we met, it was like looking at a ten-year-old, but there's so much more to you than that."

He smiled and grabbed her knee as he slipped the car onto the freeway. "Let me ask *you* something. If you could be ten again, wouldn't you grab at it? Especially if you could be ten and get paid a lot of money for it?"

Amanda nodded. It was a good point. But it bothered her all the same. Didn't people need to grow up sometime? "There are benefits to being an adult, you know."

"Name one."

"Last night, today in the shower..." she ticked them off on her fingers.

"Look," Nate said. "Up until you, sex was just sex and I never had any shortage of partners. I didn't know that it could be this different, so random hook-ups were part of the bennies for being ten, too."

"And now?"

He shrugged. "Now, I'm retiring. That makes me an old man with a gold watch. Can't get more grown up than that."

She bit her lip. "You're too young, Nate, you've got so many good years left..."

"Yeah," he said, "I do. And each year, I have a ton—literally a ton—of muscle and bone and stink that falls on me. I've broken six bones, had an uncountable number of bruises, twisted, sprained, and damaged knees, ankles, wrists, neck, ribs, and even my left hip once. How many good years is my body going to last under that every week?"

"But you love it," she said, knowing in her heart that football was as much a part of him as the scar on the back of his right hand.

Nate said nothing, just continued to drive in silence to the mall on the south end of the city and found a parking spot after nearly twenty minutes of searching.

"I'm sorry," she said, needing to break the silence as he took her hand in his. They walked across the parking lot. "It's your decision, I don't have the right..."

"Hey!" someone cried. "It's the Bouncing Broncos Girl!" Two rather large heavyset men with large smiles came running up to them. Amanda could feel Nate tense. It felt protective. Right up until she realized he seriously was preparing for a fight.

"Nate..."

"Oh shit!" The second guy was the first one to notice that there was a rather large man with his hand crushing that of the Bouncing Broncos Girl. "It's Nate Turner!"

"TNT!"

A crowd began to gather. "'Bouncing Broncos Girl' was echoed more than once. Amanda somehow managed to get her hand free and shook it to get the circulation going again. "Nate, we should..." She tried to steer him into the restaurant.

"I thought she was fucking Billy Bartock," someone said from the growing crowd. There had to be a dozen people around them by now. Mostly males.

"She is!" said another voice. "It was in today's paper!"

"Shit, she gets around!"

"Hey, Nate, you like sloppy seconds?"

Nate spun, tearing his arm from Amanda. She grabbed at him, wrapping both hands around his bicep, and tried to drag him away. Her heart pounded and she blinked back tears as she begged him to come with her.

Did Nate seriously just growl?

The crowd shifted, giving him some space. They might not have a lot of respect for TNT, but no one was willing to mess with him.

"Shit," someone said in the sudden silence. "She really is the Broncos' girl, isn't she? A pass-around girl!"

There were more than a few laughs and Nate was now in a fury, only barely restrained.

"Nate..."

He glanced at her. Saw her face. It was no longer her tugging at him. He grasped her wrist, then turned and strode through the doors of the mall, as if daring someone to get in his way, towing Amanda behind him like an errant child.

Three people scrambled to clear a path before the angry freight train that Nate had become plowed through. Two of them tangled in each other's legs and went down in a heap. Nate was now in full blown rage and she could feel him trembling as she held his arm.

"Hey, let me know when she's gone through the team and is starting on the fans," someone called from somewhere behind them, and the crowd erupted in laughter except for the occasional murmured 'shut up' that was said softly as if afraid to be heard.

Nate stalked into the restaurant next to the front door of the mall and stopped at the front desk, asking for a table for two without actually unclenching his jaw. Nate in a fury was a daunting sight. Amanda couldn't reconcile the devil that held her wrist with the quiet gentleman who had caressed her cheek less than an hour ago. It was like being a part of the Jekyll and Hyde story, and her entire body ached for the tenderness of the morning.

She wished that they'd stayed in bed, with her being snuggled, held, and protected.

"Nate," she said quietly, "you're hurting me."

He released her immediately. "I'm sorry. I just needed to get away and I couldn't leave you there." He was visibly shaking.

"Thank you for not leaving me," Amanda said, rubbing her wrist.

"I really am sorry." He glanced down at her arm. "Do you need to have that looked at?" His concern was genuine, and she did see in his eyes that he was as upset about her wrist as he was angry at the crowd.

"No, I'm sorry. I... I don't know why they called me that... well," she colored, "I do, but I was just trying to get Billy's attention, to find out where you'd gone."

"Is that what they meant?" Nate asked.

Amanda was confused. "Who meant what?"

"Them," he gestured to the crowd that had all but dispersed. The original two men had their phones out and were snapping pictures through the window of the restaurant. As they watched, a security guard showed up and shooed them off.

"What they said about you and Billy in today's papers," Nate clarified, his eyes narrowing. "You were in yesterday's paper; what's today's?"

"I don't know," Amanda quit rubbing her wrist. "If you recall, I was with you all day, so I haven't had a chance to go to a newsstand," she snapped, not liking where this was going.

He looked around and reached into his back pocket to retrieve his phone. He tapped it a few times and his face fell before becoming unreadable again. He handed her the phone.

There was a picture of her and Billy at the Chinese restaurant last night. He was leaning in. It was when he was trying to tell her he needed a beard and she was too dense to understand. It looked like they were on a tryst. She even had her hand on Billy's leg.

Bouncing Broncos Girl Bounces from Bronco to Bucking Bronco read the caption.

Amanda laughed. "Wow, if they only knew."

"Knew what?" Nate asked. He wasn't laughing.

"Nothing," Amanda said quickly. Damnit. She had to watch her tongue a hell of a lot better than this. "Nothing. Nate, Billy just wanted to talk to me. We had dinner."

"You left with him, in his car."

Amanda started to get angry again. "Wait a minute here. Please remember, Mr. Turner, that at that time I was still a hired hand. I was hired to *pretend* I was your girlfriend."

"So the beach was pretending?" Nate stepped back and crossed his arms, his expression becoming rather dark. Brooding.

"Excuse me, your table is ready!" The hostess went from chipper to uncertain in the time it took for her to grab the menus from the podium. She looked from one to the other, then over to her manager for help.

"No!" Amanda said, ignoring the interruption, "No, of course not."

"Then why did you go on a date with Billy?"

"It wasn't a date!" Amanda shoved a hand through her hair, not caring that she'd just messed up her hairstyle completely. "He just wanted to talk. That's all!"

"Wait, if you went home with him…"

"I DID NOT!" Amanda shouted, stomping her foot.

Nate stared at her. "You said he took you home."

"No, I didn't say that! But, yes, he did."

"Why didn't you drive?"

"Because your girlfriend was blocking the driveway!" Seriously, what was this, the Inquisition? He was between her and the door. Leaving was looking better and better.

The hostess had been replaced with a man in a suit and tie. The manager, from the look of things, who was fast losing patience with his celebrity guest. "I'm sorry, Mr. Thomas, if you're not wanting the table I am going to have go give it to another guest."

"I DUMPED HER!" Nate's voice carried far enough that the restaurant around them was going silent, as the customers dropped their own conversations in favor of the drama playing out in front of them.

Amanda looked at the manager. At the growing audience. She stepped in to speak, keeping her voice pitched low. "I didn't date Billy! The entire idea is ridiculous!"

"Why?"

She threw up her hands, discretion abandoned in frustration. "Because I can't tell you! That's why!"

"What?"

"I'm going to have to ask you to leave, please." The manager was no longer smiling, and the hostess appeared to be calling security.

"I was just thinking that very same thing," Nate said coldly, and stalked out.

Amanda turned to the hostess and manager in confusion. She smiled and a thought suddenly crossed her mind. *Shit! My car's still in the temporary parking lot at the airport, isn't it?*

The girl she'd seen in the mirror collapsed onto a bench as life around her resumed. A couple was seated, probably where she and Nate were supposed to be. The manager gave her a nasty look but left her alone. The wait staff kept a wary distance. Amanda didn't even bother to look up when someone took her picture with their phone.

"Is there anything I can do for you?" the hostess asked sympathetically.

"Call me a cab?" Amanda asked and fished around in her purse to root out her single emergency-only credit card. She played with it between her fingers. "Not even Bogart is going to work tonight."

She stifled a sob.

Here's looking at you, kid.

Chapter 18

"Thanks for seeing me, Coach Johnson." Amanda nervously slipped a strand of hair behind her ear. "And for coming in on your day off." She stared at the floor. She'd taken one look at him, and had decided this was the better choice. Coach wasn't happy. It was obvious from the way he had his arms crossed. Even the scowl he habitually wore seemed deeper somehow. He looked like a crude carving made of iron, someone's first attempt at making a bust, but the metal was just too implacable.

"You said it was important," he reminded her as the silence lengthened. It was amazing how quiet his office was. You'd think a place like this, right between the locker room and gymnasium, would have more sound bleeding through the walls.

You'd think there would be more distractions.

"I wanted to thank you." She swallowed hard. "You offered me a great job, and I... wasn't able to do it for you. I think I need to stay with children from now on. Less... complicated."

She glanced up to see how he was taking the news. For a moment, the iron that comprised his face softened to some degree. He uncrossed his arms. Leaned back in his chair. Relaxed. "I read the papers, too. I know you're not dating Billy."

This was the last thing she'd expected. She sat up, looked right at him. "You do?"

He smiled. "It's more than a little obvious. Billy's preferences are easy to spot, but it's never affected his game or his team."

"Billy's afraid you'll find out."

Coach shrugged. "Look at me." He stood and let his hands fall to his sides.

Amanda shrugged. "I'm sorry, what am I supposed to be seeing?"

"What do I look like to you?"

It was a test, and she still wasn't sure what he was asking. "Big, tough, scary...?"

"You know that I'm barely an inch taller than you are."

Amanda started. Coach was one of those people who took over a room just by walking in to it. He filled any space to overflowing, and if he so much as cleared his throat every conversation stopped. He was *Coach*, not just a name or a job description. It was an entity unto itself... COACH.

He was right; if she'd been wearing her stilettos she would have towered over him.

Coach sat again, reaching for his ever-present cup of coffee, and drank before speaking. "My grandfather owned a cattle ranch. He was about my size, little smaller in the gut, maybe, but it was hard living." His face softened a little. A good memory then.

Amanda nodded, feeling the knots in her stomach come loose just a little bit.

"I remember one summer I was out there to help and he had this bull. It was a ton and half of meat and muscle and had the brainpower of a hamster. That bull terrorized the entire place, no one could get near it but my grandfather. He showed up and that bull turned into a docile little baby, 'cause it feared him, yes, but also because he was a hard man. But fair. He never hurt that bull. But didn't let it be in charge either."

Amanda wasn't quite getting it. There was something profound here, she inferred that from the seriousness of his posture and the urgency with which he looked at her. Expectant, like he thought she should get it. But it was slipping past her. He must have seen that.

"You are what you present yourself. I have 400-pound professional football players who are trained, taught, and schooled to slam into each other at high speed. I have men who are young and healthy and towering over me who respect me because I command their respect. I accept that as my due. If you don't, you'll never get it from anyone. Not even children."

Amanda nodded miserably. She'd been thinking the same thing for some time, actually. If she couldn't handle one overgrown teenager in the body of a pro-football player, what did she think she could do with kids who really needed her, who needed her help?

But that wasn't the matter at hand, was it? This was about Nate. And what she'd been hired to do here.

"I don't think this is a good for me, or the team, and especially not for Nate," she said after a long pause. "I think I really just need to move on." She looked up, biting her lip. Unsure. "Please?"

Coach shrugged, though the disappointment on his face let her know she'd let him down. The knots in her stomach tightened right back up again. *Please don't let me throw up.* "You're not an indentured servant; you can leave when you like. You're an intelligent woman. It's your choice." He sighed a little as he said it.

"I don't feel very smart right now," she said, her voice barely above a whisper. "At least when you're in charge of children, you don't end up..."

"...falling in love with them?" Coach finished for her.

Amanda nodded. "It got complicated."

"So where to then?"

She shrugged. "I thought maybe I would stay at my parents' house for a while, try to figure things out from there. I need to get moved out of Nate's house. I wanted to ask you, if I could get some of the last check in advance. I ended up with a $650.00 parking ticket at the airport."

Coach blinked at that. "Where the hell did you park, a fireplug in the loading zone?"

"No, I shared a cab with Nate on the way home. I was such an idiot on the plane and, well, I forgot the stupid car was there..."

"Give me the ticket, the team will pay for that," Coach said and held out his hand. "You did get the car back?"

She nodded and rummaged in her purse until she found it. "I had to pay to get it out of the lot. It kinda took every penny I had," she said as she handed it to him.

"I'll see to it that you're reimbursed right away," he assured her. "Tell me something, though..."

Amanda glanced up from stuffing the contents back into her purse.

"You told everyone that Nate was going to retire, you shot your mouth off repeatedly on things best kept private, but if you'd told everyone that Billy was gay Nate wouldn't be jealous right now."

"You think he's jealous?" A compact fell to the floor. Followed by a feminine product that should have embarrassed her, but didn't. She was so beyond petty embarrassments right now.

"Why didn't you say anything about Billy when you had no problem telling the world about Nate?"

She shrugged, and bent to retrieve the wayward item. "I'm an idiot?"

"No," he said with a heavy sigh, "you're not an idiot, you're just acting like one. Why?"

"Because I'm not in love with Billy," Amanda cried. "I don't want to Nate to retire. Not yet! It would kill him."

Coach nodded. "So will this."

"I can't stay," Amanda said softly, dumping the last items back into the purse and standing up to go. "I'm sorry."

"I see that." Coach nodded and stepped around to the other side of his desk, hand outstretched to shake hers. "Thank you for your time and efforts. You'll be missed. Be safe."

Amanda stood her ground. Her mouth opened and closed and the room started to swim through the tears that gathered in her eyes. Her throat was dry and she found she was trembling. A part of her had thought he would fight her, beg her, force her to stay. A part of her wanted him to. She would have taken the coward's way out, and stayed and made things worse if he had fought her. But instead he stood there and shook her hand like the whole thing meant nothing. He truly was an immovable object.

Amanda bolted. She fled through the building and out to her car and there found sanctuary, a hole in the chaos that was her world. There she wept.

After a while, a heartbeat, a lifetime—it was all the same—she started the car and wiped her eyes.

It was time to go home.

Chapter 19

"Well, Ms. Jones." There was nothing friendly about the woman behind the desk. She had hair that had been dark at one time, run through with iron-grey streaks, pulled back so tightly from her head into a bun that it was a wonder her features weren't distorted all out of proportion. Somehow the woman even managed a frown, brow creasing and nose wrinkled up like she'd just seen something disgusting on the bottom of her shoe.

Sadly, she was staring at Amanda.

The sun blazed outside of the window and Colorado Springs traffic sliced past the window in silence. The laughter and screams of children permeated the building and Amanda noticed that Mrs. Klinger had, in addition to the two adult seats on Amanda's side of the desk, two smaller, child-size chairs.

She wondered for a moment what it would be like to be a child that size, called into the principal's office having sit almost under an imposing desk and facing an authority figure who was scowling at you. How kind of Mrs. Klinger to show her *exactly* how it felt.

"I see you've not yet earned your Master's," said Mrs. Klinger with a wet smack of her lips. It was like that old comic that her father used to love, the one that pronounced punctuation. Every time she got to a period, *smack*.

"No, ma'am," Amanda replied, fidgeting with her skirt. "I'm working on it. I plan to finish before the end of the year."

Mrs. Klinger nodded and glanced down at the résumé once more. Somehow, Amanda knew that if she'd been holding a blank sheet of paper, she would have paid as much, or in this case, as little attention to what was written there. "Well, Ms. Jones, thank you for your résumé. We'll be in touch."

"Mrs. Klinger," Amanda said carefully, not ready to leave just yet. Not until she knew precisely what she'd done to merit a don't-call-us-we'll-call-you response. "I realize I don't have my Master's yet, but I was hoping I could start maybe as an aide, or a temp until I graduate. I'm very close to—"

"Thank you, Ms. Jones. We'll be in touch."

Amanda stared at her for a moment, too stunned at the woman's abruptness. She stood slowly, the hawk-faced woman watching her every motion. "Mrs. Klinger, I don't know what I did to offend you, but whatever it was it was very unintentional."

"Ms. Jones." The woman sniffed. "Parents place the care of their children in our hands. Some of these children have special needs and sometimes are not able to understand the world around them. To be perfectly honest, no one wants to explain to a child why he or she is now in the hands of the 'Bouncing Broncos Girl'." *SMACK.*

Heat burned instantly on her cheeks. "That... was media-propelled. I had *nothing* to do with it," Amanda spat out the words one at a time. "I was trying to get someone's attention."

"And so you did. Thank you for your application, Ms. Jones, but perhaps you need to reconsider your profession. At the very least you need to reconsider your first choice for a venue to work in. Have a good day."

With that last *smack*, she turned to the mountain of papers on her desk. Apparently, Amanda ceased to exist for her.

She walked out of the office, trying not to look at anyone.

Outside, a child yelled, "You're from the paper!" and Amanda pretended to not hear him, scurrying past at a fast walk. Wishing she hadn't had to park almost two blocks away.

"No one even READS newspapers anymore!" she screamed at the city and watched a sheath of old papers blow past as she reached her car. One of them, a self-portrait of one of the older students, complete with smiling mother and father and a big X over what was presumably a baby brother, blew under her car, lodging against the tires.

Amanda watched as it flipped and gyrated in the breeze, but she didn't reach down to rescue it, just let it stay there, flapping helplessly under her car. After a moment, it was carried away on the wind and headed off to the mountains.

She unlocked her car and sat heavily. She gazed out the window a long time, staring at nothing in particular. She absently stared at her phone also. There was a hate mail from Jennifer in her inbox, her former roommate, accusing her of poaching the football player from her even after she'd put out. Jennifer also mentioned that she long suspected Amanda's frigidness of being an act.

"Frigidity," Amanda corrected automatically and set her phone down.

Nothing from Nate.

Nothing from Coach.

Nothing.

She sighed. Everything sucked right now.

It was a three-hour drive back to Denver, back to the guest house where her empty boxes sat waiting for her to fill. She took a deep breath and put the car into gear. On the trip, she tried to determine which state she wanted to move to. Maybe it was only Colorado that had branded her; maybe somewhere there was a city that needed a qualified teacher and didn't know that she'd been photographed with her breasts bouncing in the air, hands waving like an idiot.

Maybe.

Still no email from Nate.

Nothing.

She was alone. Or maybe she'd never felt this alone before.

She pulled into the driveway as the sun set and the house lights flickered on. Driving past the front door and around to the guesthouse in the back, she decided that Alaska was probably her best bet. No one there would care about The Broncos. No one there would care about Nate Turner.

Well, except for maybe one. If she moved there, at least someone in the state of Alaska would care about Nate Turner.

There was a lot of packing to do, mostly books. Her thesis awaited attention; her life, such as it was, had been paused, and she had a great deal to do before it would start again.

Ben and Jerry had patiently waited for her. DVD player on, and Sam began singing "As Time Goes By." She finished the ice cream and the movie, and her phone still didn't ring. Nate didn't call like the last time Sam sang. She didn't run to his house and fly into his arms. She didn't have the greatest sex of her life—again. The greatest night of her life had come and gone. Now forever a memory.

The credits rolled. The movie ended, and her life impatiently waited for her to do *something*.

So, she curled up in a ball on the couch, and eventually fell asleep while crying.

Chapter 20

Amanda stood in the middle of the living room, looking around one last time. It was a nice little house, though 'little' in this context meant smaller than a mansion. The rental truck was full and ready to go; her father had flown up from The Springs to drive it while she took her car.

Her father had been equal parts impressed at the mansion, star-struck at the idea that his little girl was working with Nate Turner, and horribly appalled that his daughter was working with Nate Turner *and* living in his guesthouse.

He kept his recriminations to himself, thankfully, at least after an initial explosion that emphasized his opinion of Troubled Nate Turner. He hinted strongly that any girl foolish enough to get caught up with someone like that was going to get burned, but after seeing the crestfallen look on his daughter's face he simply held her to him and said nothing more.

He was in the truck now, waiting for her so they could drive down together in a caravan of sorts. She made the pretense of checking once more for anything she might have forgotten. She had all the time in the world. They were gone again, the entire team heading for a game in Texas. This time she had begged off with a headache, though in truth there was no one to beg off to. Coach knew she was leaving, Nate couldn't have cared less, and Billy... Billy would find out on his own and then he'd have to find a 'Beard' who could actually play the part.

And Amanda?

She reached out to touch the couch, remembering the one just like it in the living room of Nate's big house. The night when everything seemed to be bright, and there was a future, and it looked like someone had cared for her.

It was a sharp and painful memory, not because of the way it happened but because of the way it ended, the spectacular explosion where everything shattered so publicly. Ironically, it was the one thing that the papers missed completely.

"Give me this," she said to the couch. "I was hired to keep him out of the papers, and I did. Even if I had to put myself there instead."

Feeling maybe just a shade less of a failure, she walked into the bedroom, checked under the bed, in the drawers, in the bathroom, all over to be sure that she had left nothing behind. She hadn't. There was no longer any evidence that Amanda Jones was ever a part of Nate Turner's life.

She sat on the edge of the bed and fought the tears that welled back up again. Dammit! Hadn't she cried enough?

Deep breath. Fight it. You're already at the bottom, things can't get any worse. Deep breath. You can do this. The worst is over. You only need to pull yourself together. Time to climb up from the bottom.

Besides, if she was inside much longer her father would come looking for her. The last thing she wanted was to have him find her like this. She forced herself to look at the door, concentrate on the door, the design of the wood, the minutiae. She pretty much had it shut down when the phone rang. She reached into the back pocket of her jeans and pulled it out.

"Hello?"

"Hello, is this Amanda Jones?" a crisp voice on the other half-asked, half-demanded.

"Yes?"

"Ms. Jones, my name is Lawrence Adams. I'm the General Manager of the Denver Broncos. How are you today?"

She pulled the phone away from her ear and stared at it. The caller ID said "unknown", which wasn't helpful in the least.

Okay... So, the General Manager of the Denver Broncos wanted to talk to her? "Uh... I'm alright, thank you." She felt her eyebrows almost touching, and made an effort to relax the tension from her forehead. "What can I do for you?"

"I was hoping you could come by my office tomorrow. I'd very much like to meet you."

"I'm sorry," Amanda said quietly. "I think you should know that I'm no longer with the team."

There was a very long pause. "Ms. Jones, you were never a part of the 'team', as you put it. You've never been on the Broncos' payroll and, in point of fact, have never been an employee of the franchise."

She blinked several times. "But I was hired to be..."

"Perhaps we can discuss this tomorrow; would 10:00 work well for you?"

"Uh... I guess?" She pressed her fingers to her temple, trying to still the throb that was building.

"Excellent. I'll expect to see you then."

Amanda stood, staring at the 'call ended' screen on her phone. Her stomach heaved and for a moment she thought she might lose it entirely.

She'd thought she'd already hit bottom.

She'd been wrong.

She shivered even though it wasn't cold at all. Suddenly it didn't matter if her daddy came in and found her crying.

In fact, it might be kind of nice.

Chapter 21

Amanda had thought all the offices of the Broncos were in the gym, kind of something like out of the movie where the smelly locker room had a smelly office where old men sat in sweat pants and baseball caps, chomping on cigars and spitting out names of ancient players like obscure profanity. For Coach, it was kind of true, albeit she'd never seen him smoke a cigar.

However, this... was unexpected. Except for the team logo on the wall behind the receptionist, it could have been any accountant's office in Denver with a breathtaking view of the mountains. Amanda cooled her heels in an oversized chair while a woman of indeterminant age, with skin so tight Amanda was momentarily tempted to play a drum solo on her hollow cheek, busily typed away.

When she first arrived, Amanda explained she had an appointment and gave her name. The woman had raised one eyebrow so high, Amanda was afraid the skin would snap and roll up like an old-fashioned window shade.

While she waited, paging through glossy magazines filled with forgettable sports trivia, she caught the receptionist stealing glances and creasing her brow as if deep in thought. It probably wasn't a wise move, not with skin that tight. It set Amanda on edge. She was being examined and judged, and wasn't coming up smelling so good.

Something beeped and clicked on the desk. The receptionist pushed a button and spoke into her headset, too low for Amanda to make out the words. The fact that the woman kept staring at her while doing so was more than unnerving. Especially when at the end of that conversation, the receptionist only said, "Ms. Jones, Lawrence Adams will see you now."

Amanda knew full well there had been a hell of a lot more conversation regarding her than a simple "Send her in."

She checked her watch. 10:25. She'd arrived early. He knew that full well, and was still trying to put her on edge. Or he was pretending to be a doctor and wanted to make her wait because he was busy.

The tight-skinned receptionist with the perfect business suit led her back past a cube farm to a large set of doors with the words *Lawrence Adams* stenciled on them. She knocked once and opened the door, her gaze sliding over Amanda one last time like she was looking at a particularly disgusting new species of insect.

Amanda's chin shot up. No way in hell was she going to let the skinny bitch get to her.

She stepped through into the inner sanctum and the door slammed shut behind her, making her jump slightly. Apparently there was no way in hell the receptionist was going to allow the likes of Amanda to show the least bit of confidence.

Obviously, they were at an impasse.

The room felt massive. Why did powerful men feel the need to have such massive spaces? It was like approaching the king on his dais. The plush carpet was thick enough to make walking in stilettos a challenge, much like wearing high heels on the beach. An unfortunate analogy that brought to mind her own beach experience, leaving her blushing as she crossed to where two chairs waited opposite the despot of the Denver Broncos.

"Ah, Ms. Jones," Lawrence Adams said as he stood up from behind his desk. She noticed he didn't offer to shake her hand. "Please, have a seat." He indicated one of two chairs set in front of his large mahogany desk. It put that edifice between them, making this a very official meeting indeed.

He was surprisingly ordinary in looks. Prematurely bald, with unlined face and tasteful goatee, he could have been any man seated at the bar watching a game. For all she knew, that's how he spent his Sunday afternoons, masquerading as one of the people. No suit, just an ordinary button-down shirt and dress slacks. She had no doubt that both pieces of clothing probably cost more than her entire wardrobe. They were probably designer. Wouldn't a man of this nature wear things that were designer? He sat down and smiled at her. It was not a welcoming smile. It was predatory and... she wasn't sure what was mixed in there... indulgent, perhaps? No, those eyes... it was the eyes that told the story. There was something cold and calculating in those dark eyes, like they saw right through her to her deepest, darkest secrets.

"Would you care for water, or coffee, perhaps?"

"Nothing, thank you," Amanda replied politely. The last thing she wanted was the receptionist from hell to return. Giving her the opportunity to spit into her water bottle was just asking for trouble. Besides, she was already figuring out this game. She'd studied psychology for four years, thank you very much. She was getting the feel for him. Everything here was about power. Control.

Her jaw tightened. *I haven't done anything wrong.*

He leaned forward in his chair, elbows on the desk, folded. His entire body projected affability. Kindness. Except for those fucking creepy eyes.

"I won't keep you long, Ms. Jones. Thank you for taking time out to come and see me. I've spoken at length about you to Frank."

Frank? She couldn't think who he meant and suddenly she had a glimmer of hope that maybe this whole meeting was nothing more than a big mistake. She relaxed marginally, going so far as to actually sit in the chair and quit balancing on the edge. "I'm afraid there's been some kind of mistake. I don't know who you're talking about."

"Frank Johnson." He paused as his eyebrows rose. "Head coach of the Denver Broncos?"

"Oh! *Coach.*" Coach Johnson. Amanda smiled, forgetting the gravity of the situation, forgetting even why she was there in the delight of figuring out his name. "I never knew his first name."

"No, I don't suppose there was much of a reason for you to." Adams gave her a rather condescending grin. A grin that didn't bode well at all for whatever was coming next. Amanda felt the hairs on the back of her neck stand straight up. In unison. It was an odd sensation. "Let me share some numbers with you." Mr. Adams drew several papers toward him, though his eyes remained on hers as he spoke. "The Denver Broncos have an annual revenue of about $400 million. We have an operating budget of about $85 million. This is generated through ticket sales, yes, in part, but not a large part. Most of the revenue comes from merchandizing, and the greatest share of *that* comes from family-friendly sales. Toys, children's clothing, sports equipment. That sort of thing." He leaned back and regarded her coolly. "Now, while it's true there is a certain association with some male demographics that are generally considered... high hormone, we are and we will always be a family-friendly franchise."

He waited. Amanda understood she was supposed to say something here, but for the life of her she couldn't figure out what it might be. "Okay." She settled on that. For now.

He reached into a drawer and pulled out a newspaper which he carefully laid out in front of her. "So having a 'Bouncing Broncos Girl' doesn't really fit a family-friendly environment." He smiled again, but this time there was no pretense of friendliness in it. "I saw that and laughed, assuming it was simply a fan who couldn't control her own tits. It happens, but then..."

Amanda's ears began to burn. Had he seriously just said that?

"I saw this." He pulled out the paper with her having dinner with Billy. "And found that you have been dating one of my team." He pulled out another. "Then I find out you're dating one of my players while living with another. I own this team. So, what am I to do?" He stared at her a moment. "I confront Frank Johnson and find out you were hired to escort Nate Turner, live in his house, give him the whole girlfriend experience. While it's not your fault that you stepped out on him to be with another man, I find that simply hard to believe. You simply couldn't *help* yourself?"

He threw the newspaper clippings down on the desk, sending papers flying in all directions. He was nearly yelling now. "I will NOT lose the family-friendly franchise we have carefully built up over the years for a paid escort who cannot keep her panties on!"

"HOW DARE YOU!" She leapt to her feet, slamming both her palms down on his desk, leaning in until they were nose to nose. She wanted to scream. She wanted to smack him across the face. To do something, *anything*, that would mess up that perfect smug look on his perfect smug face. "I have never in my life been so insulted, so badly mistreated!"

"Really?" He leaned in until looking in his eyes became a surreal experience that went from seeing two eyes, to really seeing only one. She could feel his breath on her face. He'd had tuna for lunch. "Perhaps I owe you an apology. If you can tell me you didn't sleep with Nate Turner, I will humbly apologize."

Amanda's throat closed.

"Perhaps having dinner with Billy Bartock was a misunderstanding? You didn't go on a date with him despite the evidence to the contrary?" He picked up that particular newspaper and shoved it toward her.

She stumbled backwards, putting both hands up as if to shield herself from the accusations. The paper tumbled onto the floor between them, the picture of herself, seated so intimately in a way that couldn't be explained without ruining someone who didn't deserve to be ruined.

Mr. Adams wasn't done by long shot. He came around the desk, encroaching on her space, cornering her against the chair though he never so much as laid a hand on her. "Can you tell me that you did NOT, in fact, take money to pretend to be Nate's girlfriend, or that he was benched until someone with *zero* knowledge of the game or the franchise deemed he was fit to play? Can you tell me his decision to quit had nothing to do with your influence, or that you have not interfered with his personal life in the form of other romantic relationships?"

He waited, his chest heaving as he stood staring down at her.

She had nothing to respond. Nothing to defend herself with. He was wrong. But he was right on every count at the same time.

She hadn't seen it coming, hadn't realized that her life could be picked over so thoroughly in a mere handful of words. She fell more than sat in the chair, hands balling up into fists though who or what she wanted to hit right now was open to debate. Was it the fault of the paparazzi who'd hunted her down with a vengeance and had so utterly destroyed her? Was it Nate's fault for...well, for being Nate? Or her own for allowing herself to get so carried away, so caught up in all of this that she'd ignored her own responsibilities? Namely the reason she'd been hired in the first place—to keep Nate out of trouble. Shouldn't that have also included keeping herself out of trouble and not falling right into the TNT insanity?

Mr. Adams stared at her long and hard while she blinked back tears and tried to think of something she could say that would absolve her, or at the very least make him stop yelling at her.

He's right. On every count. I've got nothing.

He had to have read the defeat in her eyes, in the way she slumped, trying to become one with the fabric of the chair so she could disappear. He simply gave her a look, every bit as contemptuous as the one she'd gotten from the receptionist, or from that bitchy principal at that overpriced private school. If he hadn't been more of a gentleman she suspected he would have spit at her feet, like out of an old Western. Instead he merely turned and walked around his desk, and seated himself as if tirades of this nature were everyday occurrences.

For all she knew, they were.

He didn't so much as look at her. Instead, he started gathering papers, speaking as if making idle conversation. "Frank Johnson has been relieved of his position. You were hired by him, *paid* by him and him alone. You are not and have never been an employee of the franchise and we will in no way support, back, or acknowledge your presence. You've presumably been paid by Mr. Johnson. You will not expect to see a penny from any other source. You will disavow your relationship with this franchise or you will feel the effects of a large law firm." He tapped the stack of documents on the edge of the desk, aligning them carefully and clipping them together. Only when things were neat and tidied away did he look at her again. "Did you really think he would turn away a supermodel for you?" He scoffed. "Stick to the profession you know best, and don't get involved. And above all? Do not return here ever again. Or I will have my legal team on you so fast you won't know what hit you. I'll put a restraining order on you if I need to. Do I make myself clear?" When she didn't respond fast enough, he raised his voice and repeated, "Do I make myself clear?"

"Yes, sir," she said, barely whispering the words.

He smiled. "Mary will validate your parking on the way out. Have a nice day, Ms. Jones."

Epilogue

Nate's phone exploded into plastic and glass shrapnel, spraying the locker room. Amid shouts and a few careless death threats from his teammates, he kicked the locker hard enough to dent it.

"All right, Nate," Coach Saunders called from his new office. "If you've got that much piss in you, suit up and take it out on the other guys."

"I thought I was *benched*!" Nate shouted, the last word coming out on a sneer, letting the new man in charge know precisely what he thought of him and his coaching skills. Not that Saunders had anything to do with the original order. Nor that Nate ever had any real argument with him. Saunders had been the assistant coach of the Broncos for ages.

"Good!" Saunders snapped, sticking his head out and giving Nate a thumbs-up that actually included his thumbs. "Keep talking like an idiot, but save it for the press. In the meantime, go win a football game."

"What the hell did you just say?" Nate took a step toward the smaller man, drawing himself up to his full height which gave him a good head on Saunders.

Saunders took a half step backward. "Look, they love it when you act like an ass, great. But when you're on the field, I want you focused on the game! You're starting. I know you're not sharp, but you do have skills. Use them. Be a clown later."

"Are you calling me stupid?" Nate growled, unaware that the room had gone silent around him.

"You have to ask?" Coach Saunders turned to include the rest of the room. "Listen up! Turner is back in action and will be starting. I know he's rusty, but he's been to the practices. I want you to team up, follow, and go out there. Kick their asses."

Nate stood stock-still, the blood draining from his face. He felt a large hand slam down on his shoulder, staggering him.

"Welcome back to the game, man," Billy said with a grin that showed all his teeth, and a couple of gaps that were still recent enough to not have the bridgework done.

Nate shook him off. "Just... leave me alone!"

Billy backed off, hands up.

He was almost instantly replaced with Nick, who stood there with his hand out for a high-five for several long seconds before he realized it wasn't coming. "C'mon, man, it's good news!" he said, dropping the hand and turning it into a hearty clap on his shoulder.

Nate was staggered a second time, and came up swinging.

His fist caught Nick square in the shoulder.

In moments, the room erupted into chaos, with a couple of guys hanging off of Nate and the others pulling Nick out of reach. Someone tried to put their hand over Nate's mouth and he wound up pressed against a locker, held there by five teammates who used to be his closest friends.

"Not you, too," he groaned when he relented, and slumped in their grip. They backed away warily, looking from him to the coach's shut door.

"Do you wanna get benched again?" Nick asked, his voice pitched low, but furious. He flexed his arm muscles, testing the range and motion, making sure the shoulder still functioned. "Look, I don't mind getting whaled on if it's for the game, but you don't hit your own teammates, man. I thought we were friends."

"Sorry, Nick," Nate muttered, bending to pick up his mouth guard from the floor, staring at it in disgust. "Who the hell tracked dog shit in here?"

"Nate...you need to know—"

"Billy, I don't need to know anything from you." He glared at his teammate. "I'd advise you to keep your distance, or you never know what might happen on, or off, the field." Nate shoved past him, heading for the sinks and wondering if anything was going to get that mouth guard clean enough to even consider wearing again.

Billy made as if to reach for him, then thought better of it, suddenly becoming very interested in the contents of his locker—on the other side of the room.

Nick joined Nate at the sink, which was either brave or incredibly stupid depending on how you wanted to look at it.

Nate glared, hoping to send him scurrying, too, but Nick wasn't having it.

"Enough," he said soft enough so that no one around could hear. "Enough. I don't know what you're getting all bent out of shape about. You can't blame Saunders for thinking you're a fool; you've done your best to stay in the papers as a buffoon, and you know it. We know it. Denver knows it. You created yourself, so don't get pissed if we all fall in line."

Nate looked at him. "What do you mean?"

"You know what I mean," Nick spat back, "You play the fool, get drunk, laid, blow off the rules that the rest of us have to live by, and people laugh and buy tickets. You're not here for the game. If it ever meant anything to you, it was a long time ago."

Nate waved him off. "That's bullshit."

"Is it?" Nick asked. "You fry a goat on my damn driveway, and people laugh and say, 'fuckin' Nate!' You bang girls barely legal—including my sister, I might add—swim naked in public fountains and laugh it off. Coach tried to get you to be a player, it got him fired. You pissed about Coach getting canned? They did that to get you back in the funny pages where people could laugh at you again."

Nate lunged for Nick a second time, but Nick saw it coming and grabbed him. They stood, each grasping the other's shirt, face to face. "Why are you pissed?" Nick pressed. "It's what you wanted."

"Not this." Nate said, biting off each word like it was something that tasted bad in his mouth. "I didn't want this."

"You want her," Billy said from behind. Nate flinched and let go of Nick's shirt. "I don't know what you're thinking, man," Billy continued. "I didn't 'date' her. She's not my type. I just needed a woman's perspective. I met with her, as a friend of a friend."

Nate stood, trembling with unspent energy. "I want Coach back." Not caring that Saunders heard, who'd just come out of the office in the last few minutes and was standing right behind Nick. Their eyes met in the mirror, Saunders without apology. Nate with a great deal of rage.

"Then put this on," Nick said, tossing Nate's jersey to him. "And explain to them why they should care what you want."

Do I even know what I want?

Nate stood a long time, one hand holding the mouth guard, the other holding the jersey. Every man in the room was watching him, waiting to see what he would do.

Boy or man, now?

Nate looked up at Nick. He met Billy's eyes in the mirror.

Very carefully he turned the water off, and threw his mouth guard in the trash. In silence he pulled on his jersey and moved to his locker, to find the spare mouth guard tucked away on the top shelf.

Saunders grinned and called out to the team, "Dallas is the top-ranked team this year, they're—"

"Going down," Nate finished for him. He slammed his fist into the metal facing of the locker and dented it. "They're going down *today*!"

The men around him roared and shouted, stomping their feet and setting up a din loud enough to be heard by the good people of Denver eight hundred miles away.

"Welcome to the Broncos," Billy said, thumping Nate on the shoulder, a friendly hit. His face creased in a predatory smile that, if the other team had seen it in this moment, would have had them turning tail and running all the way home to their mommies.

All they needed was a little push in the right direction so they'd know which way to run.

And Nate was going to show them where to go. He was going to show them all.

"WELCOME TO THE BRONCOS!" he yelled, head thrown back, fist raised in the air.

Damn, it felt good to be back!

The cheer was picked up by the team, one by one. It was carried with them as they ran from the locker room through the long tunnel that led them out onto the field. When the Denver fans saw him on the field they went wild, screaming and shouting his name. TNT was back and ready to play.

But the players' own shouts overrode even that adulation, and one by one the calls from the crowd changed until they took up the battle cry that had started at one locker and was carried, not by one man, but by the team as a whole.

"Broncos! Broncos! Broncos!"

Nate stood out on the field with the rest of his team. Not a little way apart as he had previously. Close in, with the rest of them.

It felt good. Right.

His heart was pounding in his ears, but his eyes were clear, and he felt sharper than ever.

They were going to kick some ass.

He wondered if she was out there somewhere. Watching.

To Be Continued...

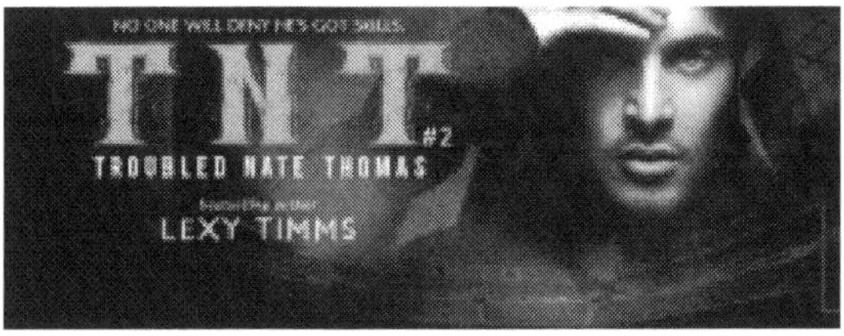
TNT
#2
TROUBLED NATE THOMAS
LEXY TIMMS

NO ONE WILL DENY HE'S GOT SKILLS.
TNT #2
TROUBLED NATE THOMAS
LEXY TIMMS

T.N.T #2 Description

Growing up is hard to do.

The infamous Troubled Nate Thomas, aka T.N.T., has seen himself the way the world sees him and it isn't pretty. While he's set on reinventing himself, his own teammates are sabotaging him at every turn. After all, where would the Broncos be without their dynamite? It seems the only person who was willing to give him room to be a better person is Amanda, but she's caught up in her own drama as she reassesses her own career goals.

United they stand, divided they fall. By reaching for each other, can they weather storms of rumor, betrayal, and the return of a first love?

The game's not even half over, the score's tied, and there's a halftime show in the works that promises to blow the lid off everything. But you have to expect explosions when you're playing with TNT.

** EXCERPT INCLUDED **

T.N.T Book 2 – Chapter 1

Nate watched George Fields running. Damn, he was friggin' fast. He covered the ground in those great long strides that just ate the ground. Poor Tim Grimes was trying to run too. Where George was a galloping gazelle, Tim looked liked a maddened bull blocked from his goal by three men who were in his way. George sprinted to the end of the field.

And Tim... well, he was trying to tear the head off one Nate Turner.

Nate forced two steps away to the side as the maddened bull threw off his stumbling blocks—Nate's teammates—and Nate's arm fired the football.

A couple of hundred years ago, someone discovered that a gun would shoot further and more accurately if grooves where cut into the barrel and thus cause the bullet to spin. This was called "rifling" The tighter the spin, the further the bullet traveled, the more accurate the shot. This was also true with a football.

Nate's spin would have made the Winchesters proud. It was tight and fast, and it flew over the head of Tim Grimes who was now too close and too fast to stop. While Nate made history, he could only see the white jersey with the word GRIMES followed by an extreme close-up of a clump of grass that tried to enter his face mask and tickled the end of his nose. The rest of the world watched a spinning ball fire through the air like a guided missile that landed in the center of George Fields's chest.

The roar of the crowd sounded good. Like George hadn't messed it up. Nate was still eating dirt and trying to wait patiently for someone to climb off Tim, so Tim could finally remove his elbow from Nate's kidney. It seemed to take forever, time Nate spent listening to the roar of the crowd and trying to figure out just which side they were shouting for. *The pass was good. George grabbed it. I saw him reaching...* What he'd done with it from there was still a mystery to Nate. He shouted questions no one heard, or ever would hear if the big oaf on top of him didn't get off soon.

Finally, the weight disappeared, and a hand reached to pull him to his feet. It was his buddy, and teammate, Nick who pulled him upright, and slapped him on the back hard screaming the word "FANTASTIC!" directly in Nate's ear.

"He caught it?" Nate asked, trying to see down the field, but the word GRIMES still blurred in his eyes, like the afterimage from a camera flash.

"Touchdown, man!" Nick yelled.

Nate whooped, blinking and trying to clear his vision. He thought he saw Nick smiling so big he was about to split his face in two parts. Or it might have been two Nick's. Possibly four.

Nate grabbed the man's shoulder. "Lead me back!" he said, wobbling a moment as he tried to walk. At least his legs worked. He'd have a bruise or six of 'em, not that it mattered. He'd come off the field with worse. It was the light-headedness from the tackle that concerned him, that could keep him off the field for the remainder of the night if they thought he was concussed.

Nick sat him down next to Coach Saunders who tried to high-five his sudden star player, but Nate missed it. Between the vertigo and the word GRIMES, he barely saw the bench, so the high-five landed somewhere in the vicinity of his shoulder. Saunders turned with the suddenness of a bird determining that the better feed was somewhere else as the defense took the field, shouting for the team doctor to get over there.

Nick stuck by his side as the old sawbones flashed a light in Nick's eyes and checked reflexes. "You alright? Pupils are even, no dilation."

It was all he could do to keep from tossing the doctor out onto the field and seeing if he could get him half as far as his last pass. "I told you I'm fine," he said as the man put a blood pressure cuff over Nick's arm and reached for his stethoscope. "I've been hit worse. That guy has a personal vendetta against me."

"Yeah," Nick agreed with a laugh. "I think he likes you. Want me to slip him a note a recess?"

Nate cracked open a bottle of water and christened his friend with it. Nick yelped and knocked Nate off the bench hard enough to send the doctor rattling against the wall behind them. The doc gave them both a dirty look, declared Nate fit to play, and scurried out of the way muttering imprecations under his breath. Most of them involving Nick's parentage.

Nate laughed, and pulled himself back onto the bench just as the Chargers snapped the ball. This time the rampaging bull was on his side. Billy was as much on his game as Nate was. He tore through the line like the defenders were little more than an inconvenience. Billy wasn't particularly fast, but once he got moving, he wouldn't be stopped by anything short of a brick wall. A reinforced brick wall.

All too soon, offense was back on the field. Coach Saunders pulled Nate aside to issue last minute instructions. Nate made a point to ignore all of them. He shifted impatiently, making all the right noises until they were motioned to take the field. He half-jogged to catch up with Nick, his head throbbing with the motion, but his vision clear at any rate. He passed Billy on the way. "Hey, how about giving us a chance to catch our breath over here?" He wasn't joking as he said the words.

"You're getting old!" Billy called back grinning. Billy grinning was a scary sight.

Not that Nate noticed. He was getting real good at not avoiding Billy as much as possible. For the last week, he'd made it an art form.

"You can't keep avoiding the guy?" Nick asked Nate as they moved out onto the field.

"I'm not. I just spoke to him."

"A necessity. That's the only time."

Behind them the crowd was going wild. It built like thunder echoing off the mountains, the stomping of thousands of feet hitting the stands, the roar that became a wordless wail of just...sound. He thought he heard his name, a TNT in there, but it might have been wishful thinking. What quarterback didn't want that attention? The notice. The acclaim.

Nate loved it. Every last bit of it. He waved at the people in the stands, clowning a little for the cameras sure to be on him after his last pass until Nick shoved him to get his attention.

"Yo, Nate...you didn't answer me."

Nate shrugged. "What d'ya expect me to say? I'll talk to him when I have something to say."

Then it was time for the next play. Nate motion for a huddle, calling the plays quickly.

The huddle broke. Lines formed. The damned word GRIMES was still etched on his forehead, actually Grimes was all he noticed. Sure, there were plenty of other players on the field, but the wearer of that particular jersey offered a gesture in his general direction that made it pretty clear that he wanted a replay of Nate's last time on the field.

Like I'm going to make this easy for you.

Nate shouted numbers, the ball was snapped back into his hands. He looked for a runner, but what he saw was Grimes. He was being held, but not by much. It was 1st and 10, they were on the 20, no one was open, Grimes broke through the line and Nate ran.

If George ran like gazelle, Nate was nearly as fast. Nate, on the other hand, had the ability to high-step his way around the writhing bodies of large men who were slamming against each other just to smash the quarterback. He broke through the line, feeling Grime's hand clutching his shirt and put on all the speed he could find.

Someone landed on his legs and he went down. Inside the line. Touchdown.

Hurt like hell again, but it was all good.

"Hey, how about giving us some time to rest over here?" Billy called out as he jogged back onto the field.

"Don't be a baby!" Nick shot back as he slapped Nate's shoulder. "Mind your elders!"

"Great job, Nate!" Coach Saunders nodded as they jogged in. "But that wasn't the play I called in."

It was the play Nate had discussed with the team though. Followed through to perfection. No way in hell was Nate telling Saunders that. Saunders was an idiot. "There wasn't anyone open! It worked," he said, with an airy wave of his hand. He grabbed a Gatorade and drained the bottle dry in a couple of gulps.

"Play the way I tell you to," Saunders snapped.

Nate threw the empty bottle in the recycling. With precision. Hard. "Even if we lose?"

Saunders swore and moved in front of Nate, getting right in face. "You want to go back on the bench?"

The Chargers made the next down, followed by a whistle blew. It was the end of the first quarter.

Nate and Coach Saunders stared, unmoving.

"Nate," Nick said slapping his friend on the shoulder and dragging him away. "Come on, dude. Let's grab a drink?"

Nate shook his head. "I just had one." He looked over his shoulder at Saunders and then back at Nick. Billy was coming his way and he tried to turn, but Nick's grip on Nate's forearm tightened. "No, QB. Billy's your friend. Deal."

"Is he?" Shit. Too late to walk away.

"Dude, did you hear it?" Billy was nearly jumping with restrained excitement. "They're calling you TNT."

"So? Some damn paper made that shit up and I got saddled with it years ago."

"Not for 'Troubled Nate Turner'," Billy said, beaming. "I just heard it from a reporter on the sidelines. Now they're calling TNT for the bombs you throw. You set a Broncos record!"

"That throw to George?" Nick asked. Billy nodded. "How long was that?"

"91 yards!" He held up a hand to high-five Nate who stared at it for a long moment.

I just threw a 91-yard touchdown? There were maybe a dozen men in the history of the game who'd made a 99-yard completed pass, but in the Broncos, no one had ever done more than 90.

It was worth celebrating.

"Nate," Nick sighed, and gave Nate a look so pointed, he could have staked a vampire with it.

Nate returned the gesture and Billy's hand caught his and held it. It was like looking at a child's hand rapped in an adult grasp. Billy pulled Nate to him and the smile vanished. "Dude, I found out that she was hired to run interference for you. I wasn't trying to move in on you, I swear to it. I didn't know you loved her. OK?"

Nate wrenched his hand away. "Who said I 'love' her?"

"You do, every time you look at me like I just kicked your dog. I'm sorry, I didn't know. I promise you that I did not *ever* try anything with her." Billy hesitated, glancing down at his feet. "She's... not my type."

"Something wrong with her?" Nate heard himself saying.

"You would rather I made a move?" Billy snapped, his head coming up, dark eyes blazing.

"Enough!" Nick yelled and lowered his voice as other team members started turning their heads to see what was going on.

"Enough. Nate, you're not pissed at him. You're pissed at her. You're fuckin' missing her too so you're being an asshat."

Nate spun on the other man, but Nick was having none of it and met his gaze square. After a minute, Nate lowered his eyes and turned away. "Doesn't matter," he mumbled.

"Get her back," Billy said like it was the most obvious thing in the world.

"After the game," Nick added quickly with a sudden panicked look at Billy.

"After the game," Billy agreed.

Nate turned and walked past Saunders without acknowledging him.

"*Asshat*?" Billy asked Nick while watching Nate. "Please tell me that's not a thing."

"What?"

T.N.T. Book #2 – Chapter 2

"Amanda," her mother said in that long-suffering tone that set Amanda's teeth on edge. "Are you even listening?"

"I'm trying to Mom!" Amanda tried to keep the exasperation out of her voice with little success. "I've been here less than a week, can it wait till the game is over? Please?" She never once took her eyes from the screen. There was no way she could, not with Nate on the field. She stared at his number, willing him to turn toward the camera. To do something that would let her get a glimpse of his face.

"No, young lady, we need to talk now."

There was a certain steel to that tone that told Amanda that her mother was done screwing around. Amanda muted the game and set up to record, all the while fuming that she was a 22-year-old woman, not some child. Something her mother couldn't seem to get through her thick head.

As she turned away from the TV she saw the pass from the corner of her eye. Everything else forgotten, she stood and cheered, jumping up and down.

"Stop that this instant!" Her mother stomped her own foot and had to rescue several knick-knacks from an end table that threatened mass suicide by means of throwing themselves over the edge. "Are you quite finished?" she asked, paying no attention to the fact that it was her own stomp that had upset the table. "Do you have any idea how much crap I had to take about that horrible nickname you gathered?"

"Bouncing Bronco Girl," her father added helpfully from his armchair, eyes still on the screen.

"Thanks, Dad." Amanda threw him a grin over her shoulder, ignoring her mother who exhaled noisily and rolled her eyes – a feat somewhat akin to patting one's head while rubbing one's stomach at the same time.

"Yes, *that* one. Listen, dear, I DO understand. Don't think that I don't. I know about wild passion." She looked askance at her husband who looked away, suddenly very interested in the remote Amanda had abandoned on the end table. He shook it a few times and went so far as to take the batteries out and put them back in again.

"MOM! I do NOT need to know this."

"It was before... that doesn't matter. The point is, I *do* understand. But it didn't work out. You ended up in an untenable position, darling, and now it's time you move on."

"Mother, I... Wait, 'before'?" Amanda shook her head, really not wanting to hear the answer. "It was a job. I was hired to keep Nate out of the papers, to help focus him."

"Yes, dear, and you did that by putting yourself in the papers and letting the world see your..."

"Enthusiasm?" her father tried, rapping the remote on the end table, as it genuinely no longer seemed to be working now.

"Breasts, Simon, her breasts! You gathered that horrible name and everyone I know spent the next week talking about it. I'm simply trying to save you the embarrassment."

"Her?" Simon asked, then shrugged when no one seemed inclined to clarify. He took the batteries out again.

"Mother, it was nothing I did. I was trying to attract attention... never mind, I heard it as I said it. I was trying to find Nate, I was with George! Your nephew."

"I know, Mary called me the other day, dear, George is still trying to find his car."

"Amanda," her father said slowly, putting the remote down again. "This Nate has a reputation... for being a bit of a lothario." He looked up at her intently, in that way that made Amanda's stomach turn, like she'd been caught doing something she shouldn't. Though this whole situation was far beyond stealing cookies from the cookie jar.

And then there was his word choice. "'Lothario'?" Amanda finally asked as the word hung out there overlong.

"It means a womanizer, dear," her mother said, batting Simon's hand away from the remote as he reached for it again.

Amanda blinked. "Yes, Mom, I know what it means, I just never thought I would actually hear it."

"So," her mother continue, giving Amanda's father a quelling look guaranteed to keep him silent until she'd said her piece. "You had a fling with a football player. We've all done things we regret and you've become another conquest for this Nate person. Fine, it's over and behind us all. However, your father and I have been talking..."

Amanda guessed how much "talking" her father did.

"We have decided that we cannot in good conscious continue to pay for your school," her mother said in a rush. "It was one thing when you were living on campus and things were a bit more discrete, but events have spiraled out of control. You have only to submit your dissertation and you will have your Masters, if you want your doctorate, you will have to manage that on your own."

"But..." Amanda sank down into the chair next to her father's. On the screen football players did that complicated little dance that let you know they'd scored or done something equally important. She didn't see Nate. "I don't even know if I want to pursue my Masters at this point."

"Of course you do dear," her mother corrected her with a cluck of her tongue.

"You need to finish the degree, kitten," her father added in his slow deliberate way. "If only to..."

"You're close enough to the degree that it would ridiculous to leave at this point. It was your decision to follow in my career..."

Follow her mother's career? *You have got to be kidding me.* Amanda had genuinely been interested in the development of the mind, in what made it tick. The decision to pursue child psychology had been entirely her own, for her own reasons. The idea of being able to guide the growing mind had captured her own imagination in her studies from the time she'd first learned about Mary Ainsworth and Jean Piaget and their exploration into the various stages of a child's development.

The fact that her mother was a fairly eminent psychologist had absolutely nothing to do with anything.

She opened her mouth to explain just that but as usual, her mother beat her to it.

"Of course you chose a different path, working with children. What I don't understand is why you changed those goals once *again* and became a babysitter to a footballer with Peter Pan syndrome and classic narcissistic tendencies."

"I think your mother..."

But Amanda's mother was on a roll now, with too much forward momentum to notice what anyone else was staying. She stood directly in front of the TV, perfectly positioned so that all you could see was a bit of the ref on one side of the screen. "You're unfocused, dear. You're all over the place. You need to figure out what direction you want to proceed. There's absolutely no point to going back to college and spending all that money when you have no idea where you're going."

"Though you're welcome to stay..."

"Here," her mother finished in triumph. All that was missing was the end zone dance. "But you will concentrate on your dissertation first and foremost and you will earn your keep, as the saying goes."

Amanda flinched. "I tried to find a job, mother, but—"

"You tried to find a job with children, my dear," Her mother said airily, obviously proud of herself for some reason. That reason, whatever it was about to unloaded on them all, and

Amanda dreaded the very thought of it. "You've already walked away from that path. Why would anyone hire you for it?"

"She was always good with kids, Margery,"

"Please, Simon, don't interrupt."

Simon raised his hands in defeat and grabbed the remote again as soon as he attention was off him.

Margery turned the loving basilisk gaze back to her daughter. "No, my dear, you'll be coming to work with me in my clinic."

"At the VA?" Amanda's mouth fell open. "Will they allow that? I don't exactly have the degree yet."

"You're not going to come in as a full-fledged counselor, my dear. Every VA is scrambling for volunteers. You'll simply be another one on the docket. I've already arranged it. You'll report directly to me, and in that way I can keep an eye on you. And that means," she grabbed the remote from her husband's hands, smacked it once on the end table, and switched the TV off. "No more of this ridiculous waste of time. And no more of that... person. Is that clearly understood, young lady?"

"I..."

But Amanda was talking to an empty space her mother had just vacated.

Amanda's father motioned her over to his chair. Amanda hesitated and then finally came and sat on the arm of his chair the way she used to when she was twelve and the universe wasn't treating her fairly. His arm came around her, and she rested the cheek on the top of her head.

Maybe some parts about coming home weren't so bad after all.

Her dad tugged her hair until she leaned down, so that her head was even with his own. "It's going to be OK," he whispered, planting a kiss on her cheek.

She sat back and looked at him skeptically. He smiled softly, patted her hand, then got up and wandered off toward the kitchen.

END OF EXCERPT

TROUBLED NATE THOMAS

T.N.T Series

Part 1
Part 2
Part 3
COMING DEC 2016

UNKNOWN IDENTITY SERIES #2
unpublished
BESTSELLING AUTHOR
LEXY TIMMS

Find Lexy Timms:

Lexy Timms Newsletter:
http://eepurl.com/9i0vD
Lexy Timms Facebook Page:
https://www.facebook.com/SavingForever
Lexy Timms Website:
http://lexytimms.wix.com/savingforever

More by Lexy Timms:

Book One is FREE!

Sometimes the heart needs a different kind of saving... find out if Charity Thompson will find a way of saving forever in this hospital setting Best-Selling Romance by Lexy Timms

Charity Thompson wants to save the world, one hospital at a time. Instead of finishing med school to become a doctor, she chooses a different path and raises money for hospitals – new wings, equipment, whatever they need. Except there is one hospital she would be happy to never set foot in again—her fathers. So of course he hires her to create a gala for his sixty-fifth birthday. Charity can't say no. Now she is working in the one place she doesn't want to be. Except she's attracted to Dr. Elijah Bennet, the handsome playboy chief.

Will she ever prove to her father that's she's more than a med school dropout? Or will her attraction to Elijah keep her from repairing the one thing she desperately wants to fix?

** This is NOT Erotica. It's Romance and a love story. **

* This is Part 1 of an Eight book Romance Series. It does end on a cliff-hanger*

Managing the Bosses Series
The Boss
Book 1 IS FREE!

Jamie Connors has given up on finding a man. Despite being smart, pretty, and just slightly overweight, she's a magnet for the kind of guys that don't stay around.

Her sister's wedding is at the foreground of the family's attention. Jamie would be find with it if her sister wasn't pressuring her to lose weight so she'll fit in the maid of honor dress, her mother would get off her case and her ex-boyfriend wasn't about to become her brother-in-law.

Determined to step out on her own, she accepts a PA position from billionaire Alex Reid. The job includes an apartment on his property and gets her out of living in her parent's basement.

Jamie has to balance her life and somehow figure out how to manage her billionaire boss, without falling in love with him.

Hades' Spawn MC Series
One You Can't Forget
Book 1 is FREE

Emily Rose Dougherty is a good Catholic girl from mythical Walkerville, CT. She had somehow managed to get herself into a heap trouble with the law, all because an ex-boyfriend has decided to make things difficult.

Luke "Spade" Wade owns a Motorcycle repair shop and is the Road Captian for Hades' Spawn MC. He's shocked when he reads in the paper that his old high school flame has been arrested. She's always been the one he couldn't forget.

Will destiny let them find each other again? Or what happens in the past, best left for the history books?

The Recruiting Trip

Aspiring college athlete Aileen Nessa is finding the recruiting process beyond daunting. Being ranked #10 in the world for the 100m hurdles at the age of eighteen is not a fluke, even though she believes that one race, where everything clinked magically together, might be. American universities don't seem to think so. Letters are pouring in from all over the country.

As she faces the challenge of differentiating between a college's genuine commitment to her or just empty promises from talent-seeking coaches, Aileen heads to the University of Gatica, a Division One school, on a recruiting trip. Her best friend dares who to go just to see the cute guys on the school's brochure.

The university's athletic program boasts one of the top hurdlers in the country. Tyler Jensen is the school's NCAA champion in the hurdles and Jim Thorpe recipient for top defensive back in football. His incredible blue-green eyes, confident smile and rock hard six pack abs mess with Aileen's concentration.

His offer to take her under his wing, should she choose to come to Gatica, is a temping proposition that has her wondering if she might be with an angel or making a deal with the devil himself.

Seeking Justice
Book 1 – is FREE

Rachel Evans has the life most people could only dream of: the promise of an amazing job, good looks, and a life of luxury. The problem is, she hates it. She tries desperately to avoid getting sucked into the family business and hides her wealth and name from her friends. She's seen her brother trapped in that life, and doesn't want it. When her father dies in a plane crash, she reluctantly steps in to become the vice president of her family's company, Syco Pharmaceuticals.

Detective Adrien Deluca and his partner have been called in to look at the crash. While Adrien immediately suspects not everything about the case is what it seems, he has trouble convincing his partner. However, soon into the investigation, they uncover a web of deceit which proves the crash was no accident, and evidence points toward a shadowy group of people. Now the detective needs find the proof.

To what lengths will Deluca go to get it?

Fortune Riders MC Series
NOW AVAILABLE!

Undercover Series - Book 1, PERFECT FOR ME, is FREE!

The city of Pittsburgh keeps its streets safe, partly thanks to Lt. Grady Rivers. The police officer is fiercely intelligent who specializes in undercover operations. It is this set of skills that are sought by New York's finest. Grady is thrown from his hometown onto the New York City underworld in order to stop one of the largest drug rings in the northeast. The NYPD task him with uncovering the identity of the organization's mysterious leader, Dean. It will take all of his cunning to stop this deadly drug lord.

Danger lurks around every corner and comes in many shapes. While undercover, he meets a beauty named Lara. An equally intelligent woman and twice as fearless, she works for a local drug dealer who has ties to the organization. Their sorted pasts have these two become close, and soon they develop feelings for one another. But this is not a "Romeo and Juliet" love story, as the star-crossed lovers fight to survive the deadly streets. Grady treads the thin line between the love he feels for her, and his duties as an officer.

Will he get in too deep?

Heart of the Battle Series
Celtic Viking
In a world plagued with darkness, she would be his salvation.

No one gave Erik a choice as to whether he would fight or not. Duty to the crown belonged to him, his father's legacy remaining beyond the grave.

Taken by the beauty of the countryside surrounding her, Linzi would do anything to protect her father's land. Britain is under attack and Scotland is next. At a time she should be focused on suitors, the men of her country have gone to war and she's left to stand alone.

Love will become available, but will passion at the touch of the enemy unravel her strong hold first?

Fall in love with this Historical Celtic Viking Romance.

* There are 3 books in this series. Book 1 will end on a cliff hanger.

*Note: this is NOT erotica. It is a romance and a love story.

Knox Township, August 1863.
Little Love Affair, Book 1 in the Southern Romance series, by bestselling author Lexy Timms

Sentiments are running high following the battle of Gettysburg, and although the draft has not yet come to Knox, "Bloody Knox" will claim lives the next year as citizens attempt to avoid the Union draft. Clara's brother Solomon is missing, and Clara has been left to manage the family's farm, caring for her mother and her younger sister, Cecelia.

Meanwhile, wounded at the battle of Monterey Pass but still able to escape Union forces, Jasper and his friend Horace are lost and starving. Jasper wants to find his way back to the Confederacy, but feels honor-bound to bring Horace back to his family, though the man seems reluctant.

Now Available:

Coming Soon:

LEXY TIMMS
TRUTH
LEXY TIMMS
LEXY TIMMS
LEXY TIMMS
SPANKED SERIES
PASSION
PLAYMATE
PLEASURE
LEXY TIMMS
MOMENT IN TIME: BOOK ONE
HIGHLANDERS
Bride

NO ONE WILL DENY HE'S GOT SKILLS.
TNT
#1
TROUBLED NATE THOMAS
bestselling author
LEXY TIMMS

NO ONE WILL DENY HE'S GOT SKILLS.
TNT
#2
TROUBLED NATE THOMAS
bestselling author
LEXY TIMMS

NO ONE WILL DENY HE'S GOT SKILLS.
TNT
#3
TROUBLED NATE THOMAS
bestselling author
LEXY TIMMS

Don't miss out!

Click the button below and you can sign up to receive emails whenever Lexy Timms publishes a new book. There's no charge and no obligation.

Sign Me Up!

https://books2read.com/r/B-A-NNL-WPTL

BOOKS 2 READ

Connecting independent readers to independent writers.

Did you love *Troubled Nate Thomas*? Then you should read *One You Can't Forget* by Lexy Timms!

From Best Selling Author, Lexy Timms, comes a motorcycle club romance that'll make buy a Harley and fall in love all over again.

Emily Rose Dougherty is a good Catholic girl from mythical Walkerville, CT. She had somehow managed to get herself into a heap trouble with the law, all because an ex-boyfriend has decided to make things difficult.

Luke "Spade" Wade owns a Motorcyle repair shop and is the Road Caption for Hades' Spawn MC. He's shocked when he reads in the paper that his old high school flame has been arrested. She's always been the one he couldn't forget.

Will destiny let them find each other again? Or what happens in the past, best left for the history books?
Hades' Spawn is a 4 book series.

Also by Lexy Timms

Alpha Bad Boy Motorcycle Club Triology
Alpha Biker

Conquering Warrior Series
Ruthless

Diamond in the Rough Anthology
Billionaire Rock
Billionaire Rock - part 2

Dominating PA Series
Her Personal Assistant - Part 1
Her Personal Assistant - Part 2
Her Personal Assistant - Part 3
Her Personal Assistant Box Set

Firehouse Romance Series
Caught in Flames
Burning With Desire
Craving the Heat
Firehouse Romance Complete Collection

Fortune Riders MC Series
Billionaire Biker
Billionaire Ransom
Billionaire Misery

Hades' Spawn Motorcycle Club
One You Can't Forget
One That Got Away

One That Came Back
One You Never Leave
Hades' Spawn MC Complete Series

Heart of the Battle Series
Celtic Viking
Celtic Rune
Celtic Mann
Heart of the Battle Series Box Set

Justice Series
Seeking Justice
Finding Justice
Chasing Justice
Pursuing Justice
Justice - Complete Series

Love You Series
Love Life: Billionaire Dance School Hot Romance
Need Love
My Love

Managing the Bosses Series
The Boss
The Boss Too
Who's the Boss Now
Love the Boss
I Do the Boss
Wife to the Boss
Employed by the Boss
Brother to the Boss
Senior Advisor to the Boss
Forever the Boss
Gift for the Boss - Novella 3.5

Moment in Time
Highlander's Bride
Victorian Bride
Modern Day Bride
A Royal Bride
Forever the Bride

R&S Rich and Single Series
Alex Reid
Parker

Saving Forever
Saving Forever - Part 1
Saving Forever - Part 2
Saving Forever - Part 3
Saving Forever - Part 4
Saving Forever - Part 5
Saving Forever - Part 6
Saving Forever Part 7
Saving Forever - Part 8

Southern Romance Series
Little Love Affair
Siege of the Heart
Freedom Forever
Soldier's Fortune

Tattooist Series
Confession of a Tattooist
Surrender of a Tattooist
Heart of a Tattooist

Tennessee Romance
Whisky Lullaby

Whisky Melody
Whisky Harmony

The Debt
The Debt: Part 1 - Damn Horse
The Debt: Complete Collection

The University of Gatica Series
The Recruiting Trip
Faster
Higher
Stronger
Dominate
No Rush

T.N.T. Series
Troubled Nate Thomas

Undercover Series
Perfect For Me
Perfect For You
Perfect For Us

Unknown Identity Series
Unknown
Unexposed
Unpublished

Standalone
Wash
Loving Charity
Summer Lovin'
Christmas Magic: A Romance Anthology
Love & College
Billionaire Heart

First Love
Frisky and Fun Romance Box Collection
Managing the Bosses Box Set #1-3

Made in the USA
Middletown, DE
13 April 2017